SUMMER SORCERY

The Wizard and the Imp
Book 1

Summer Sorcery Copyright © 2021 Brandon Lim

This is a work of fiction. Names, characters, places, and incidents either are the product of the author's imagination or are used fictitiously, and any resemblance to actual persons, living or dead, events, or locales is entirely coincidental.

Published by Imp Publishing
Cover Art by Becky Salter: Wilder Ways Arts & Illustration

ISBN: 978-8384683-0-9

To Ruby

There's magic in books. Find it.
Unleash it.

The Wizard and the Imp
Book 1

By Brandon Lim

For Sarah, who made this possible,

and for our children, who made it necessary.

Chapter 1

The Accident

Elias crashed through the ferny undergrowth, scrambling to keep his footing. He ducked under a large branch, grabbed the trunk, and made a sharp left turn. *Keep going* he thought. His pulse hammered to the rhythm of his feet. *Can't catch me. Won't catch me.* He leaped over a fallen tree, skidding off the mossy bark to the other side. His shoes slid on a patch of mud. A wild look crossed his face. *Stay up, keep moving.* He twisted to the right and launched himself through a thicket of bushes, arms in front of his face but otherwise heedless of the thorns as they grabbed at his clothes.

Elias slammed to a stop. "Wow," he whispered, panting heavily as he caught his breath.

Three thudding heartbeats later he was knocked to the ground.

"Caught you, Elias!" His big sister, Nyree, cackled triumphantly as they lay in a tangled heap on the grass.

"What'd you stop for anyway?"

From his vantage point of mostly under Nyree, Elias pointed.

They were in a grassy clearing. A gentle rise from where they lay led up to a low, broken, stone wall. Some way behind this were the shattered ruins of a large building. The moss-covered remains of walls curved suggesting a round tower. Not the usual little watchtower keeps that Elias knew were strewn around the Scottish landscape – this tower had been built with ambition. The gigantic double doorway, at least three metres high, seemed small next to the crumbling stonework.

"How have we not found this place before?" Elias barely took his eyes from the ruins as he scrambled out from under Nyree and back to his feet.

"Well, it's not as if we've been here that long," said Nyree, dusting herself off.

"We've been exploring these woods every day since we moved." Elias slowly walked up the slope. His eyes roamed hungrily over the broken masonry seeking handholds and hiding places.

"Yeah, all of two weeks ago, numpty." Nyree rolled her eyes at her little brother but followed him up the hill to the ruins with a smile spreading on her face.

To Nyree the ruins felt strange. Filled with an odd peace like they were suspended out of time. On top of that was a melancholy that overtook the place like the mosses and ferns which overran the stonework. Underlying everything was an air of patient watchfulness.

She stood in the broken-down doorway. Charred splinters from the great oak doors littered the ground underfoot. She breathed in the place, enjoying the moist woody smells of the forest.

"Strange for a building so grand to be all the way out here." She murmured to herself.

"What's that?" Elias jumped down from the nook of a nearby window, startling his sister.

"You wee…" Nyree swatted at him. "Don't do that."

"Sorry, Nyree," said Elias. His grin suggested otherwise.

"I was saying that it's odd. A big building like this all the way out here." Nyree waved her arms, encompassing the ruins. "I mean, this place would have been huge before it fell down. Hard to imagine something like this not having at least some farms surrounding it. Or even a larger settlement."

"There's the whole of Dunfermline just through the woods." Elias shot her an unimpressed look.

"Well, that's my point," said Nyree, her gestures getting even more emphatic. "It's all the way through there. Like they tried to build a supporting town and missed. No, this place is out on its own deliberately. Which is odd."

"Mmm hmm." Elias had turned away, inspecting the crumbling wall beyond the doorway. He reached up for a handhold and started to climb.

Nyree sighed and left Elias to his clambering. She

turned her attention to what was left of the wrecked door. Carefully brushing back some of the dust and invading plants, Nyree could just make out carvings on the wood. Symbols of some kind. Not letters exactly, but definitely symbols. A closer look showed hints of a silvery metal delicately worked into them.

Nyree rummaged in her bag for her magnifying glass.

Elias yelped as he slipped from the inner wall. He stumbled as he landed, tripped on a fallen beam, and fell straight through the rotting door that had been hidden by a tangle of ivy.

"You alright?" Nyree dropped her bag and hurried over.

"Yeah, fine," laughed Elias. "I jumped for a hand hold. Don't know what I was thinking. Glad this stuff broke my fall though, whatever it is."

"Huh," said Nyree looking past him. "There's a stairway in there, against the main wall. I wonder if this was a broch?"

"A what?" said Elias as he picked himself up.

"A broch," repeated Nyree slowly. "You know, an iron age Scottish castle. Some folk say they were a defence against the Romans, but I think that's a bit daft, 'cos most of them have been found way up north. There aren't really many down this way at all. This could be really big, you know."

"Mm hmm." Elias nodded, although Nyree could see he wasn't listening.

Brothers made no sense, she decided. After all, he'd given her those books on archaeology for her last birthday, but for some reason he zoned out whenever she talked about it. As if anyone could not find it all fascinating. And this place… It didn't look like it had been studied before. But so close to civilisation… There was no way it could have gone undiscovered.

"I'm going to see if there's some good free-running to be had in there, okay?" said Elias.

"Yeah, fine," said Nyree not taking her eyes off the stairway.

As her brother bounded off, enthusiastically looking for trouble, Nyree started to climb the stairs.

A little way around the tower the stairs opened out onto a wide platform, crumbling at the edges. It looked like there had once been a complete floor running across the entire structure.

So not a broch after all, thought Nyree with a sigh. *Still, that begs the question: what is this place?*

She turned away from the broken edge of floor to start a proper investigation of the remains of this level and let out an alarmed squeal.

"You okay, Nyree?" Elias's voice came floating up from the ground floor.

"Yeah, just startled." Nyree gave an embarrassed chuckle. "I didn't spot this huge statue until I almost walked into it. Typical."

The statue stood next to a rectangular stone table, placed against a section of wall. It was as if the figure was working at the desk. Above the table, carved into the stone of the wall were two alcoves either side of a window so coated with grime that almost no light came through. The alcoves held the rotting remains of wooden shelves, which still carried dozens of small bottles. Surprisingly, some of them were still unbroken.

Nyree rummaged in her bag, took out her camera and snapped a few photos before stuffing the camera back in. She found her sketchbook and pencil, sat on the sun-warmed stone floor, and began to draw.

Photographs were quicker and more accurate, but Nyree found that drawing forced her to slow down, observe and take note of the details. Taking the time to study shade and shape made it difficult to miss things. Difficult, but not impossible. It often seemed to Nyree that stuff would turn invisible as soon as she was searching for it. Still, the sketching helped.

One floor below, Elias had just finished a spot of wall running. He smiled as he considered his efforts. With only a little practice he'd managed to get the entire way from one window alcove to the next without touching the ground. Of course, getting *into* the second bay was another thing entirely. So far, he had managed to launch himself off the wall four times, bash his elbow off the stonework twice, and on the final try graze his knee on the windowsill. Minor scrapes were, in his view, just the cost of results. Still, too much practice at one thing could become tedious with so many other possibilities around.

He turned slowly. The walls had crumbled enough that climbing them looked distinctly possible. The trouble was that most of the walls had collapsed at about head height. Too low to be worth it. He eyed up the rubble littering the floor and considered the building possibilities. There was plenty of material, but it would be hard work to shift. He cast his eyes upward for something to swing on.

A smile capered with a wide-eyed look of mischief across his face as a plan formed in his mind. He nodded once and set to work. First a good bit of pacing around, assessing the movability of various pieces of debris. Then some careful judging of the best location. Three minutes later his plan was under way. Ten minutes after that his ramp was taking place. After twenty minutes of happy labour, he was ready to test.

He had cleared as much rubble as he could from a strip in front of his ramp, creating a mostly clear runway. Elias stood well back, put his head down, and charged. As he hit the top of the ramp, he jumped hard and reached for the floor above.

This is going to be glorious. He grinned, thinking of how surprised Nyree would be when he popped up from the edge. *Of course, she probably won't even notice,* he thought. *All the better for surprising her.*

His reaching fingers snagged the decaying stonework of the upper floor. A pebble sized chunk broke away in his hands and he fell.

Elias was experienced in these matters, though. He'd figured on this happening, which was why he had also dragged in some small, leafy branches and a bunch of ferns to break his fall if things went less than well. He was reckless, not stupid.

11

The foliage shushed as he landed in it. Like it was promising it wouldn't tell anyone what had just happened. He lay back wearing the smile of the undefeated. Another small rock fell from the upper floor and pinged off his forehead.

"So, it's like that, is it?" he murmured to himself as he stood up for another attempt.

Nyree glanced up to check just how the bottles were lying under the collapsed shelves. A frown developed on her brow. How *had* she managed to miss that the statue was holding one of the bottles? She quickly sketched a bottle in the statue's right hand. Another glance. *Oh, Nyree,* she thought, rolling her eyes, *there's clearly no stopper in that bottle. Stop making things up or this whole exercise is pointless.*

She slapped her sketchpad down on the floor. Her frustration echoed off the wall in front of her. Nyree stood and stalked toward the statue like a kitten approaching a stray ball of yarn.

Close up, Nyree could see at least one more detail she'd managed to miss. This one was perhaps unsurprising. The bottle's stopper was in the statue's left hand. The statue's craggy face loomed over Nyree as she looked up, admiring the sculptor's attention to detail. It seemed almost alive. From where she stood, it gave her the weirdest feeling that it was thoughtfully regarding her. Like the artist had intended this piece to be viewed from that exact spot by someone precisely Nyree's height.

She shrugged. Who could explain the workings of an artist's mind? As Nyree turned back to finish her sketch she froze. A chill crept up her back to take residence at the base of her skull. *Neither the cork nor the bottle are carved from stone,* she thought, turning slowly. *Come to that, this building has been ruined for centuries. How could the bottle still contain any liquid at all?* She glanced quickly back at the bottle. The liquid within was a bright emerald green, shimmering with a swirling iridescence as if the fluid were alive.

Nyree took half a step back, hardly daring to breathe. She looked up at the huge stony face which now smiled down at her.

Elias leaped as if his life depended on it. A satisfying pain shot through his left hand as it slammed against a rough rock on the edge of the upper floor. His grip tightened and held fast, the stone staying firm and steady within. A lunatic grin lit his entire face as he grabbed on with his right hand and pulled himself up.

The bottle lurched forward. Its lurid green liquid splashed out in a chaotic arc. Nyree threw herself back. Her flailing arm smacked the bottle free from the statue's grasp. It went spinning madly toward the broken edge of the floor.

Nyree landed arm and shoulder first, rolled and scrambled to her feet. She dashed the green fluid from her eyes just in time to see the spinning bottle smash straight into Elias's face as he pulled himself up over the edge.

Red blood and green potion splashed wildly from the impact. Shouting his surprise, Elias lost his grip and fell back over the edge. Dismayed terror burst from Nyree's lungs in a furious scream. Her limbs fizzed with a sudden burst of energy sending her charging down the stairs. She drew her next breath as she fell to her knees next to Elias. Her little brother lay dazed on a heap of ferns and bracken. Blood streamed from his nose, but he seemed otherwise unhurt.

"You gave me such a scare!" Nyree shrieked at him. She slapped him on the shoulder.

"Scared *you?*" Elias huffed through the blood, "You threw a bottle at my head and knocked me off a first-floor ledge. I gave *you* a fright?

Frowning slightly, Elias dabbed at his nose, then looked at Nyree. "Got any tissues?"

He reached for the offered paper handkerchief, then snatched his hand back staring at it in wide eyed fright. Starting at his fingertips, his hand was turning blue. Not the normal, healthy blue of a white Scottish boy on a winter morning but a deep royal blue, shading to midnight around his knuckles. Faint sapphire lines snaked their way over the back of his hand and up his arm, trailing the deeper blue as it spread.

Elias could feel the tingle of it spreading up his arm and across his chest, fanning out toward feet and face.

14

He screamed. A panicked cry of distress that bubbled up from his belly until it seemed to fill the whole world. With one last stricken glance at his sister, pale and terrified next to him, Elias fled.

Chapter 2

An Encounter with Trolls

It took Nyree a moment to realise he'd left. Had she *really* seen Elias transform into a strange blue creature from a second-rate fantasy novel? Come to that, had it *really* happened because of a green potion thrown by a giant stone man? Nyree shook her head to clear it. Green fluid spattered on the stone floor next to her. The dust around it shimmered.

The scream came again, snatching her out of her daydream musings. The heart-ripping sound of a lost little boy having a seriously bad day. The cries were made so much worse by the fact that Elias, who had had an instinct for mischief since birth, usually took mishaps in his stride. Nyree shot to her feet and bolted for the door.

For the briefest moment Nyree thought she saw movement on the shattered floor above. She caught a blink-long glimpse of the statue peering over the edge. Curiosity overtook her and she turned to look properly. Then the scream came again, from further than before. Nyree's head snapped around, all thought of investigating the strangeness above crushed by her brother's panic.

Elias ran as if his life depended on it. As if the dreadful changes that had taken him could be left behind. He crashed through the undergrowth, heedless of the grasping tug of thorns, like all the demons of the underworld were after him. But there was only one monster, and there was no escaping it.

A tree loomed before him. He shifted his weight to dodge it. Too late. He braced for impact. Some deep-buried instinct chose that moment to surface. With a feline twist, he launched himself at the trunk. Elias rebounded using his hands and feet. He landed in a tight roll and resumed his wild flight without breaking stride.

The carefree boy almost returned. His wild grin started to form as he realised how cool that move was. Then he remembered why he was running. The brief distraction was enough though. His foot snagged on an unnoticed tree-root and he tripped.

Elias rolled and regained control at the brink of a small stream. He sprang to his feet and caught sight of his reflection in the glassy surface of the water. His ears, enlarged and slightly pointed, framed a face which he could barely recognise. His jaw seemed larger, or at least more solid. As he gasped for breath, he saw teeth which looked like they could bite through steel. And that blue. That blue. That deep, dreadful, unnatural, other-worldly blue. It didn't coat his skin like body-paint – it *was* his skin.

It was the eyes that proved too much to bear, though. Staring back at him from that excruciatingly alien face. Those dark eyes. Completely human and so very much his own. He screamed again.

He stumbled onward into the woods. Tears streamed from his eyes. He didn't know where he was going. He didn't care. He just wanted to get away from that face that was seared into his memory.

Elias's misery was interrupted by the shock of a sharp, short fall. With his tear-blurred vision he had failed to notice the small rock face until he stepped over it. He landed on his feet, jarring his right ankle. Muttering words that he wasn't supposed to know yet, Elias hobbled to a nearby rock and sat down, head in his hands.

"'Ello. What's this then?" rumbled a voice, deep like war-drums.

Elias shot to his feet and spun around, wincing as his ankle took the weight. He screamed again, fear overwhelming his previous upset. What he had previously taken for boulders near the base of the cliff were in fact a pair of creatures, roughly human in form. Very roughly. Their hulking shapes were covered in a coarse grey skin, green around the joints where lichen had settled. Each wore a ragged assortment of cloth. Barely more than crudely torn animal skins.

"Dunno," said the second creature, "reckon you can eat it?"

Nyree skidded to a stop at the top of the rock face. Her frantic dash through the woods, driven by the terrified cries of her brother, had almost sent her tumbling over but she stopped in time.

In the middle of the clearing below, two massive grey figures towered over Elias.

"Maybe," growled one. "Figure we should squash it first, though."

"Yeah," chortled the other, "them bones is a bit tough otherwise."

The second creature raised a vicious looking club over its head, preparing to strike. Nyree looked around frantically for a weapon. Anything that she could use to at least distract the creatures and give Elias a chance to escape. Her eyes lit on a rock – large enough to do some damage, small enough to throw reasonably well. She grabbed it and took aim just in time to see the club swing down.

There was a sickening, splintering crunch and Nyree opened eyes that she hadn't realised she'd closed.

Elias stared back at the terrible creatures. Small splinters of wood tickled down his chin and fell onto his torn, mud-stained t-shirt. He felt his jaw relax back into a more normal position.

The creature to Elias's left rumbled a growl deep in its throat. "Did that wee brat *eat* my club?"

The other chuckled evilly. "I like a dinner with some

fight to it."

"That club was new," the first creature shook its head in disbelief. "What kind of thing *eats* a club what's being swung at it?"

"Guess we can ask him while we're eating him." The club-less creature reached out a grasping hand.

Elias's eyes darted left and right as he scrambled back, frantically seeking escape. *Rock face that way – no escape there.* His gaze danced over his shoulders. *Thick bushes this way – might slow them down. Might slow me down. Come on, think. Find a way out.* He glanced again at the rock face looking for any advantage he might have missed. *Oh no.* He spotted Nyree standing at the cliff top, hefting a large rock. For all that Elias admired his big sister, coordination was not Nyree's strong suit. Probably his best chance of getting away from her rescue attempt un-hurt would be if she aimed *at him.*

As soon as the shock of Elias's impossible reprieve began to fade, Nyree raised her rock and aimed once more. *I just need to distract them long enough for him to hide,* she thought.

"Hide Elias," she whispered, pouring everything she had into the thought of him getting away from those awful brutes. She could taste her fear, feel it like a hot, angry pulsing in her chest.

Like a special effect in a horror movie, a dense mist rolled in over the clearing. Everything was shrouded in a thick, white blanket of fog. Unnaturally, the fog pooled most heavily around the two creatures hiding them in moments. From her high vantage point, she could just see Elias as a blue smudge slipping silently toward the edge of the clearing.

"Don't let dinner escape!" yelled one creature.

"I think I see something," called the other.

"Where? I can't see nuffin."

"Down 'ere, I think I've got him."

"Aargh, he's grabbed my leg!"

"A fighter this 'un. Bigger than I thought too."

"Get him off me Grot!" screamed the first creature, thrashing wildly.

"I've got 'im Grind," growled Grot. "This'll show 'im."

There was an ear shredding scream of pain and the thrashing intensified.

"Get 'im Grot. He's bit me!" Yelled Grind.

"Must've bit you when I bit 'im," growled Grot savagely. "This'll soften 'im up a bit."

The harsh crack of fist on flesh filled the mist and the sounds of Grind's distress grew.

"Idiots," muttered Elias, placing his hand gently on Nyree's shoulder. "They don't even realise they're fighting each other."

Nyree jumped at Elias's sudden appearance and stifled a yelp that might bring trouble their way. She recovered and grabbed her brother in a fierce hug, held tight very briefly, then pushed him back and swatted him on his shoulder. Her hand throbbed slightly from the force of the blow and she shook it.

"What were you thinking, running off like that?" hissed Nyree.

"You want to do this here?" Elias looked pointedly at the misty clearing where the battle sounds were starting to weaken.

"Good point." Nyree swatted him again for good measure, more gently this time, before heading back through the woods.

∞⚜∞

A safe distance away, Nyree stopped Elias with a gentle hand on his shoulder. She pressed him to sit on the moss-bound stump of a felled tree.

"You alright?" She settled on the stump next to him.

"I'm not hurt," Elias mumbled at his hands.

"Not what I asked though." Nyree hugged her brother gently with one arm.

"Do I look alright?" Elias sprang to his feet. "I'm a monster."

"Because you're blue?" Nyree sat calmly. She fought to keep her voice even.

"Because I'm hideous." Elias turned away, his voice a rasping whisper.

"Well first of all," Nyree continued, "you're really not. Secondly – that's nonsense reasoning anyway. Was that ugly old bat Mrs McColl from our old school a monster?"

"Are you kidding?" Elias spun back round. "She was the nicest teacher in the whole place. How could you call her a monster?"

"My point exactly." Nyree sat unruffled on the stump, hands clasped around one knee.

"Oh…" Elias slumped to the grass as the fight drained out of him.

"You're not a monster. Yes, your changes are…" Nyree paused to find the right word, "extreme. The way you dealt with that creature's club, though? That was awesome."

"Yeah," Elias sighed at his hands, "but I'm blue."

Chapter 3

Malachite

At Nyree's insistence, they headed back to the ruins. Nyree wanted answers, and that seemed like the best place to start looking. Besides, they needed to figure out what to do about Elias's colour. They couldn't exactly turn up at home and expect nobody to notice.

They walked back the way they had come, this time avoiding the worst thorns. Nyree kept up a constant chatter. Not about anything in particular. It seemed that she was trying to distract Elias from his blueness. Tall order though this was, Elias began to calm down.

Elias pushed through the final thicket, holding back a branch for his sister. He suddenly snatched his arm back in surprise. The branch slapped roughly into Nyree's face.

"Hey," she grouched, "watch it, would you?"

She pushed through to see Elias gazing in delight at his arm.

"My hand's not blue anymore!" Elias grinned

infectious relief at Nyree. Even as he did, he felt his ears shrink and his jaw relax back to its usual shape.

Nyree looked on in amazement as the blue drained from his skin, the swirling patterns fading to nothingness leaving no outward trace of his transformation.

"So that's over then?" Elias sounded hopeful.

"Well, I still want answers." Nyree squared her shoulders at the ruins. "Let's go find that statue."

"Find the what?" Elias gave the ruins a baleful look then hurried after his big sister.

The statue in question was now standing in the doorway to the ruins.

Definitely not a trick of the light this time.

Nyree approached it slowly but with a hungry curiosity.

"Where'd that come from?" Elias's loud voice shattered the stillness of the clearing, making Nyree jump.

"It was upstairs before. It was standing at a table that I was sketching." Nyree started circling the statue now, taking it in from every angle. "It kept moving. Only slightly, though. I thought I was just imagining it. You know me. Anyway, I went over to check some details up close. That's when it threw that stuff at me. I tried to dodge... I think I must have knocked the bottle from its hand... that was when... that must have been... then you fell. After that it's all a muddle, but I'm sure I saw it move. I think it might be alive."

26

"Indeed I am. Well met, young mistress." The statue's voice was a warm rumble, like a landslide crossed with an earthquake.

Nyree and Elias took an involuntary step back. Fascination widened Nyree's eyes. Elias's raised his fists, which were starting to go blue again. As the colour changed, Elias clenched his jaw. His hands only shook a little.

"Peace, children. I mean you no harm." The statue raised a pair of huge rocky hands in a gesture that was, presumably, meant to be unthreatening.

"No harm? You turned me blue!" Elias's raised fists were now joined by a scowl.

"Elias," Nyree spoke softly, her attention fixed on the statue, "if the giant stone man says he doesn't mean us any harm, let's not try to change his mind, okay?"

Elias nodded once, mumbled, "okay," and lowered his fists. Slightly.

Nyree, somehow noticed this without looking away from the stone giant. She released a trembling breath.

"Right then, stone-man, we need some answers." Despite being dwarfed by the statue, Nyree almost sounded in charge.

"Most certainly you do," the statue rumbled. "Let's start with introductions. I am Malachite, and I am entirely at your service. Shall we go inside and make ourselves more comfortable?"

Malachite turned and stepped back into the ruins. He picked his way through the wreckage with surprising fluidity and grace.

"I get the feeling that today is about to get much

weirder." Nyree aimed for her tone to be 'light and breezy' but completely missed.

"Easy for you to say." Elias inspected the blue as it faded out toward his fingertips.

Re-entering the main chamber was like stepping into a fairy-tale movie. All the debris and extraneous plant life was busily tidying itself up. In the centre of the room stood Malachite, calmly directing everything with the slightest of hand movements. At the snap of his fingers an assortment of rocks and ferns assembled themselves into a trio of surprisingly comfortable looking chairs.

"Please have a seat." Despite his gravelly growl, Malachite had started to sound unexpectedly gentle. "We have a lot to talk about."

"We should finish the introductions first." Nyree sat on the indicated chair, "I'm Nyree Forester and this is my little brother Elias."

"Ah," Malachite sounded like a great puzzle had just been solved, "a brother and sister. That explains everything. A sibling bond is strong, and you may need each other in the times ahead."

"How does that 'explain everything?'" Elias threw himself into his seat. He waved his blue fingers accusingly.

"My apologies young master, let me start at the beginning." Malachite sat forward, looking poised to launch into an epic tale.

"Sorry to be difficult, sir," Nyree had spotted Elias's

restless shuffle and decided to intervene, "but I think we need some things explained first."

"Yeah, like why I keep turning blue."

"And what that green stuff was."

"Apologies again mistress." Malachite settled slightly into his seat, studying his hands as he spoke. "For all the long years searching for this moment, I'm afraid I have spent little time considering how to explain it. Answers first then.

"The green potion is called 'True Awakening' and to the best of my knowledge it has been created only once in the last two thousand years. Its purpose is to awaken the magical potential inside a living soul. I attempted to dose you with it, mistress, because I saw in you that which I have long sought. The perfect balance of free imagination and scientific reason. It is this balance that is required to make a sorcerer."

"Okay but loads of people are like that. Why me? Why..." Nyree paused as her thoughts caught up. "Wait, a sorcerer?"

Malachite chuckled, a sound like dancing footsteps on a dry riverbed. "Yes indeed, a sorcerer. As for why I chose you. In all honesty, I do not know. It felt... right somehow."

"What about me?" Elias sat up, eyes shining. "Why did you choose me?"

"To my shame I have to say, I did not." Malachite sighed.

Elias slumped in his chair, his eyes welling up. Nyree felt a pang of pity. All the stress of the accident, and then to be told that, once again, he was the tag-along little brother. Nyree had been chosen and he had not.

"You misunderstand me, young master," Malachite hurriedly continued. "Looking, as I was, only for a sorcerer, I lacked the wisdom to see the potential within you for what it is. You were chosen by the magic itself. A potion as powerful as True Awakening has a life and a mind of its own. At its core, magic is vitality and consciousness. The greater the magic, the more of each it must have. When my first master created it, some of his intentions would have passed into the potion, allowing it to choose with more clarity and wisdom than I."

"Thanks," Elias sniffed. "But I'm not a sorcerer, just a blue freak."

"Do not be so quick to judge," said Malachite. "You are most certainly not a sorcerer. At least not of the usual kind. It appears that the magic has touched you more deeply. I must confess that I do not fully understand your transformation. Indeed, had I not seen with my own eyes, I would have doubted that such a thing was possible. No, this will take careful consideration to judge properly. What we know now is: unique – almost certainly. Blue – this is, occasionally, indisputable. Freak – do not think it for a moment."

"Exactly." In that moment Nyree started to love this strange stone man. She smiled over at Elias. "We'll figure out the details, but just think about the possibilities. The way you took off and ran through the woods was quite something. How you dodged the trees! Impressive doesn't cover it. Not to mention how you bit clean through that creature's club!"

Elias managed a weak smile, "Yeah, the club thing was cool."

"Creatures?" Malachite sat up sharply. "What creatures? Where?"

Nyree described the creatures and their run-in with them. Malachite nodded slowly as he absorbed Nyree's tale, interrupting occasionally to clarify details.

"Well, that is news indeed." Malachite's warm rumble took on a hard edge. "First of all, well done. The fog which hid your brother was the result of your first conjuration. Not an easy one either. I believe there are great things ahead of us. Secondly, the creatures you met were hill trolls. Vile beings at the best of times. Usually, they lurk in sheltered areas in the hills, waiting for hapless victims to take refuge from a storm. I have never heard of them venturing so far from home before. I wonder…"

"Wonder what, Malachite?" Nyree and Elias asked together.

"Nothing to worry about." Malachite didn't sound convincing. "I think, though, that I should pay these trolls a visit. Anyway, you two have had an exhausting day and the hour already draws late. You should go home now and rest. Tomorrow we can take your first proper steps into the world of magic."

"Before we go," Nyree made no move to leave, "I think we need to know what we were chosen for? If the True Awakenings potion is as rare and powerful as you say, your master surely had a plan."

"I believe he did. My master was the last guardian,

set to watch for a great evil. As his time on Earth grew short, he searched for another to take his place. None were suitable, though he scoured the world. So, he created me, a man of stone, who could watch forever for the right person to carry on his task and guard against the great evil."

"What evil?" Elias leaped to his feet, his cheeks flushing blue.

"Elias, calm down. Malachite is trying to explain." Nyree's voice trembled slightly as she spoke. This was that point in all her books where the hero's life changed forever. Despite her nerves she didn't want to miss a moment.

Malachite sighed like the wind in a graveyard, "In truth, I don't know what evil."

"You what?" yelled Nyree and Elias together.

Chapter 4

Faeries

Malachite closed his eyes and sighed deeply. He sat motionless for brief moments that felt like years to Nyree. Not the slightest movement betrayed what thoughts could be churning in his great stone head.

At last Malachite broke his silence. "Strong though he was, my master could not survive the magic he used to create me. With his dying breath he told me a prophecy. 'In the age of all knowledge, wisdom will be found. Through strength and weakness, a power will rise and halt the theft of souls or bring about the end of all who know.' He said only that, then pressed the potion into my hand and whispered 'Choose, Malachite.' He died with those words on his lips. I have spent my time since trying to understand the nature of my task and find someone worthy of my master's gift."

"You poor thing," whispered Nyree. "Alone in the world with only that to guide you."

"So, you chose us," said Elias, "to somehow fight an unknown evil soul stealer, or possibly just kill everyone? Not to mention that you turned me blue. And you call this a gift?"

"I am sorry, children," breathed Malachite, "but in essence, yes. I believe that you are the raw material to become the heroes foretold."

"But what if we're not?" asked Nyree. "What if we 'bring about the end' instead? I'm starting primary seven in…" she bit her lip, counting how long until the end of the holiday, "six weeks. I don't think we're set to cover soul-thieves any time soon. Saving the world definitely doesn't come up until at least high-school."

"Patience, children." Malachite sat straight now. "The evil is not yet upon us. We have time. I have awakened the power within you. In time, I will train you to use it well. When the evil finally does rise, we will be ready. As for 'bringing about the end'. Try not to worry yourselves too much."

"Try not to worry?" Elias began to turn an agitated blue. "You're serious?"

Malachite's frown deepened, and he drew another long breath. "I'm sorry. I should be clearer. My understanding of the prophecy is that the evil must be defeated. We can't just ignore it until it goes away. The prophecy has lost a great deal in translation, and seers are a strange bunch at the best of times."

"What do you mean, translation?" asked Nyree.

"Well, it was given to me fifteen hundred years ago,"

rumbled Malachite, "and to my master some long time before that. The beginnings of English were barely an idea back then, and as alien to what we now speak as Russian or Chinese. There is guidance to be had in the message of those words, but not the words themselves."

"You've been here since 500AD. By yourself?" said Elias.

"Well, no," admitted Malachite, "not just here, and not always by myself. I have travelled the world searching for clues and arming myself for my task."

"You went around collecting weapons?" Elias sat forward, his eyes widening. "Where are they then?"

"In here," Malachite pointed to his head. "I am armed with knowledge. The wisdom of ages and the magics of many peoples and many times. It is this that I shall give to you."

"Cool," whispered Nyree.

"So, no giant catapults then?" Elias's disappointment was written all over his face.

"Young master," Malachite answered with a grin, "I can show you a dozen different ways to build them, then have them launch spears of lightning. I am armed with knowledge."

"Cool," agreed Elias.

"Now enough talk for today. I must investigate these trolls, and I have much to prepare. Tomorrow we will begin your training."

"We need to get home, anyway," said Nyree. "Otherwise Dad will start to worry."

Elias flicked a glance at his watch. His eyes snapped wide. "Mum will be home from work soon, then we'll all get in trouble."

The next morning Nyree and Elias were up at first light, excited to begin learning from Malachite. Breakfast was a hurried affair. A bowl of cereal gulped down in silence. The used dishes clattered in the sink as they hurried to get going, although Nyree paused for a moment to start the coffee machine before heading for the door. She liked doing the little things that seemed to make her parents happy. In return, it seemed Mum and Dad let her get away with a bit more than Elias. Of course, Nyree liked to think that she'd do it anyway.

"Bye Mum," called Elias as he barged past her in the hall. "We're off to the woods."

"Okay kids, have fun," came the answer, then in a quieter voice: "Nyree? Could you try to stop your brother doing anything too reckless, please?"

"Sure Mum." Nyree gave her Mum a quick hug on the way out. "By the way, coffee's on."

"Oh, you are a star!" Mum smiled, giving Nyree an extra hug. "By the way, does Dad know where you're going?"

"I left a note in the kitchen for him. He doesn't need an early start, just because we're having one."

Nyree's mum raised her eyebrows. "I think your dad might see it differently, but okay. Have fun. Be safe."

The forest hummed with more life than before. Obvious, even as they raced through it. The biggest change, which stopped Nyree in her tracks, was at the stream that led to the tower. Only yesterday morning the stream was merely a run of water wandering down the hill. Today it was bursting with life. The water pulsed with energy. Brilliant shimmers of insects flitted around on the surface. The occasional fish flashed through the water. Above the surface, a tiny light danced busily. Elias ran on for a few paces, before realising that his sister wasn't following.

"Come on Nyree!" yelled Elias over his shoulder without breaking his stride.

"Yeah, I'll be right with you," murmured Nyree. She felt captivated by the dancing light and thought she could make out something at its core. Nyree had no intention of being right with him. "This is amazing…"

Nyree stumbled closer to the light. She tripped over tree roots and bracken but didn't dare take her eyes off it. As she drew nearer the speck of light resolved into a tiny glowing woman, barely larger than Nyree's hand. Her body gave off a faint glow that sparkled off iridescent wings, which flickered frantically as she darted about over the water.

"You're beautiful…" whispered Nyree.

The tiny woman shrieked and whipped around in the air. The russet brown messenger bag slung over her shoulder bounced off her hip and tangled in a wing. Nyree reached out to catch her, but the woman landed in the stream with a gentle plop.

Nyree leaned over the water and fished the woman out as quickly as she could.

The woman coughed vigorously. "Just look at this—" She coughed again. "Absolutely ruined."

"Are you alright?" Nyree leaned lower, trying not to loom too much over the poor creature.

"Yeah, I'm fine. I'm just a bit wet—" The tiny woman slowly looked up at Nyree. She bit her lip and her eyes widened sharply. "Oh, this is bad. This is very bad, Faltha. You've done it this time."

"It's alright," said Nyree softly. "I'm not going to hurt you. Really. I'm Nyree." She offered a hesitant hand, then hastily withdrew it, frowning at herself. "Faltha, is it?"

"I'm not scared." Faltha stood and tried to straighten out her soaking dress. After a moment, she gave up and turned back to Nyree. "Despite how it looks, I can actually take care of myself. But we're not meant to be seen by humans. Not anymore anyway. Not since the wizards all died out." She brushed some of her long red hair from her face with the back of her hand, streaking mud across her forehead as she did. "Shame you're not a wizard. That would save me a lot of hassle."

"Well, I kind of think I might be, actually."

"Don't be silly, child," scoffed Faltha. "The last of them died over a thousand years ago."

"Yeah, Malachite said something about that."

"Wait, you're serious!" Faltha zipped into the air in a spray of muddy water. "Malachite's gone and done it?

38

You're the one?"

"Um, yeah, I guess…" Nyree's face started turning a little pink.

"As in: 'In a time of doom, one will come forth. Chosen and gifted with magic. She will save us all or bring our end.' That one? Seriously?" Faltha was hovering at Nyree's nose now. Her glow intensified in her obvious agitation, which made Nyree blink and flinch away.

"Well, the one Malachite told me sounded a bit different, but yeah. That was the idea, I think." Nyree sat back to see Faltha properly. "Kinda scary stuff actually."

"Huh, I suppose so. It doesn't really feel like a time of doom though. Hadn't thought about it to be honest. Oh! One moment…" Faltha darted off and grabbed a floating thistle seed out of the air. She appeared to listen intently for a moment, then dropped the seed and flew back to Nyree.

"What on earth was all that about?" asked Nyree.

"Oh that," Faltha chuckled like the tinkling of glass beads, "I'm a wish gatherer!"

"You grant wishes!" whispered Nyree in awe.

"No silly," laughed Faltha, "I don't have the power for that. I just gather them up. Listen to them. If there are any that I think really need granting, I suppose I'd pass them on to someone at Court. That's rare though. Sit, please." Faltha gestured at a fallen log.

"Why on earth do you collect them then?"

"Well, the wishes children make are important." Faltha settled on Nyree's knee. "That's better. If we're going to chat, I might as well get comfortable."

"Important?" prompted Nyree.

"Oh yes, umm." Faltha dragged her attention back. "Not so much the wishes themselves, as what is wished for, and how many wishes are made. A wish is a declaration of belief, you see, and belief is what makes the magical world work."

"What, like in Peter Pan? If someone says they don't believe, a faery drops dead?" The idea that a stray word could kill her new friend worried Nyree.

"No, nothing like that. No, belief is power. The more a faery is believed in, the stronger they become. The problem is, though, belief is a finnicky thing. If there's too much belief, or too little, ordinary people start to get interested. Then investigations happen and before you know it folk start 'collecting samples' and cutting them up to figure out how they work."

"That sounds horrible!"

"Yeah, the Enlightenment was a tough time for us faeries." Faltha shuddered, her light dimming for just a moment. "Thankfully, people seem to be getting on a bit of a mystical kick at the moment. Certainly, there's plenty of wishing going on. It's a shame so many are for new gadgets."

"Well, some of them *are* kind of useful..." mumbled Nyree. She was halfway through pulling her camera out of her pocket as she spoke. Guiltily biting her lower lip, she slipped it back in.

"Anyway," said Faltha fluttering, "I need to tell the Court about you. Will you wait for me? I'll be back as quickly as I can".

Faltha shot off into the forest. Nyree sat down to wait. She pulled out her note pad and began sketching everything she had just seen.

Chapter 5

The Imp

By that time, Elias had reached the tower. He was vaguely aware that Nyree wasn't with him but too excited to properly worry. Malachite was waiting at the crumbling doorway, still and lifeless as a sculpted rock. Nothing happened. Elias started to think he'd dreamed everything.

Then Malachite spoke. "Welcome back young master. Will your sister be joining us?"

"She was just behind me a moment ago." Elias looked over his shoulder, wondering what was keeping her.

A bird fluttered into the clearing and landed on Malachite's shoulder. It chirped its cheerful song 'chiff-chaff, chiff-chaff'. Malachite responded with a strange sound, like the wind whistling through a canyon. The bird responded with a shrill chirp. Malachite made the sound again, and Elias realised that he was speaking to it. The bird cheeped again briefly and flitted off beyond the treeline.

"She's fine," Malachite rumbled. "Apparently, she's sitting next to the stream, not far from here. She's sketching in a notebook."

"Yeah, she does that." Elias rolled his eyes. "She can spend hours like that when something new catches her attention."

"Well, we can get started at least," said Malachite. "I was hoping to speak to you first anyway, as your transformation has proven to be," he paused to consider, "startling."

"Hmph. Startling. That's one word for it. It's just not fair! Nyree gets to cast magic spells and stuff, and I change colour and become some... creature!" As Elias got more worked up, his skin started to take on a blue tint again. "I can't even control it!"

"You can, you just don't know how yet," Malachite began, but Elias cut him off.

"It's not a joke, don't make a joke about it! This is my life. I turn blue! I don't know what to do." A hint of defeat invaded Elias's voice. "What am I?" he finally whispered.

"You are yourself. Nothing more, and certainly nothing less," said Malachite as gently as a large, talking statue can manage. "I was not making a joke. All my life I have travelled the world, studying sorcery, and searching for answers. Hoping to find clues to help us defeat the enemy. I have never fitted in, wherever I have been. So, I have never learned what it is like to suddenly stop fitting. I cannot teach what I have not learned. Yet that is the task I am given. Please bear with me and I will do my best."

Malachite paused, his stony face showed a hint of hope, betrayed the slightest edge of desperation. Elias nodded slightly. Once. He couldn't look at Malachite.

Malachite paused a moment longer. Finally, he said: "As for what you are, if you need a label, 'imp' would not be unsuitable. But in truth, you really are nothing but yourself. Your true self. A magical manifestation of your innermost being if you will."

"Hold on. A what of my who now?"

"Manifestation… sorry. What I mean to say is the magic has looked at who you truly are, what it is that makes you do what you do and say what you say. It has taken that and made it physical. Given it body and form."

"Yesterday I bit through a troll's club in mid-swing and swallowed it like it was a biscuit!" Elias started turning blue again. "What has that got to do with my inner self?"

"Patience, Elias." Malachite's tone was an essay in forced calm. "This is a complicated thing, and a magical thing. It doesn't always make sense at first. Magic follows rules, but not like a computer, more like a lively but well-behaved child. Magic follows the rules, but it gets creative, pushes the boundaries, tries its best to find the loopholes, the gap in reason, the opportunity to be beautiful, or terrible… or both.

"In your case, you say you can eat improbable things. Let me ask: do you like food?"

"Well, a boy's got to eat," Elias shrugged.

"Are you fussy about it?"

"No, I'll eat almost anything… oh!" As understanding dawned, the blue tinge faded from Elias' skin.

"Yes, now you see." The satisfaction was clear in Malachite's voice now. "Who you are determines what you can do. And so, you can see that while I can show you the way to learn, only you can teach yourself how to be you."

"But I still can't control it!"

"Nor can any of us control who we are." Malachite sighed with the sound of a landslide. "Do you think your sister chooses to get distracted in the woods? Do you think she chooses to be so fascinated that she loses herself for hours in her sketchbook? If we pay attention and learn who we are, if we are wise, and listen to those that have more experience, then just possibly we can learn how to use that to our advantage."

"You sound just like my parents." Elias smiled at the thought of this huge rock creature being anything like Mum or Dad.

Malachite laughed. "And if one day we meet, that might not be the only thing we agree on!"

∞⊰✦⊱∞

Nyree put the finishing touches to her drawing of Faltha with the thistle seed. A slight rustling by her ear snatched at her attention.

"That's wonderful." Faltha giggled. "Do I really look like that?"

"Pretty much," Nyree turned to see her new friend. "Although, I've not done your wings any justice. They are amazing. I don't think pencil can capture the shimmering colours at all."

Faltha flittered about looking slightly flustered. "Anyway, I'm back now. Obviously."

"Yes, I was meaning to ask. Back from where exactly?"

"Well, the Seelie Court of course… oh, sorry, I keep forgetting how new you are to all this. Poor thing, you really don't know anything, do you?" Faltha finally settled on Nyree's sketch book, gazing at the drawing.

Nyree smiled slyly, then let out an exaggerated sigh. "If only someone wise could tell me all about the Silly Court. Maybe Malachite would know. I should probably go see him."

Faltha shot upright, her attention snapping away from the drawing. "Well first of all it's Seelie. S-E-E-L-I-E. Secondly, I know a hundred times as much as that old gravel-heap."

"I don't know why I didn't think of that before! Faltha, would you tell me about the Seelie Court?" Wheedled Nyree, hoping she wasn't overdoing it.

"Certainly!" Faltha beamed. "Sit yourself down… oh." She noticed, as if for the first time, that Nyree was in fact sitting. "Well, then we'll begin."

Faltha drew herself up to her full ten centimetres, hands clasped behind her back glowing with pride from her very core. Nyree stifled a giggle at the sight of this imposing school master who could fit on her hand. Faltha scowled for a moment, daring Nyree to laugh, then moved on. "The Seelie Court, the Shining Throne. We are the guardians of all that is good and beautiful in the world. We are the faery court of old, formed to keep order in the magical world. We settle disputes, keep the peace, and uphold the laws. Above all we nurture and protect all things beautiful in the world. 'Beauty is Life' is the highest principle of the court."

"So, nothing ugly deserves to live? Attractive people can do no wrong? Is that what you stand for?" Nyree was horrified. After less than a day in the magical world, was she seeing a foul truth below the sparkling surface?

"Not even a little bit!" Faltha seemed genuinely distressed now. Her iridescent wings flicked dazzlingly. "Pretty doesn't mean beautiful, and beauty isn't always pretty. We Seelies know that, although, perhaps, this wasn't always so. Beauty is…" She trailed off looking around for inspiration. "Beauty is context. A bubble! Shimmering, flickering colours in the sunlight. Beautiful, yes?"

"Uh, yeah, I guess so."

"Well, when it's used to amuse a child, in a game, for a party, then it is. What about when it's landing in your dinner, or on some clean laundry? Speaking of which, a line of laundry flapping in the breeze. In its way that's beautiful too. The simplicity of living with the world, just using what it offers without capturing, harnessing, or diminishing it at all."

Nyree was smiling now. This she could get behind. This sounded like the faery folk she had dreamed of. "Are they all like you? The faeries?"

"Ha! No. Even within the Seelie Court, we're all as different as different can be. The faery folk, as some

48

legends would call us, aren't really a single people at all. You could say that it is a term for all the creatures of magic. So, there are water sprites, like me, and of course the other sprites. We tend to look pretty similar, and I suppose we're what most people think of when they think of faeries. But there are many others."

"Trolls, for example?"

"Yeah, though not that nice an example. They're certainly not part of the Seelie Court!"

"Too stupid I expect," mused Nyree, thinking back to her encounter with them. It already seemed more distant than only yesterday.

"Too stupid, and just simply ugly inside and out," replied Faltha. "Faeries of the court are all beautiful, of course. The more beautiful, the higher our position at court."

"You must be very important then." *Flattery perhaps, but a friend at court could be worth having*, thought Nyree.

"Oh, if only. I'm really one of the lowest. That's why they have me all the way out here gathering wishes. 'Keep out the way Faltha, would you please?' 'Try not to break anything!' 'Just shoosh now little one!' No, I'm not important at all. That said, I seem to be moving up in the world."

"Really, how's that?"

"Well, you just happen to be looking at the new Court Emissary to the Tower! Can't believe I didn't tell you sooner!" Faltha spun around with glee, her wings taking on an extra glow.

"The Tower!" Nyree stood up quickly, grabbing her sketch pad from under Faltha. "I forgot! Elias will be wondering where I am! I have to go."

∞⊹∞

Nyree was expecting to see Elias sulkily waiting for her by the door. Instead, she was met by Malachite's stony back, his head tipped up as if gazing at the crumbling stonework.

"Nyree, look what I can do!" Elias's excited voice floated down from above.

Nyree looked up and there, near the top of a two-storey section of wall, was her brother. Elias's skin was shining a deep royal blue, his clawed fingers gripping the stonework as he scrambled quickly around the remains of the tower.

"Good!" Malachite growled approvingly, "Now jump!"

"No!" Nyree screamed.

"Whee!" With a yell of pure joy Elias sprang from the wall, arms outstretched. He seemed to hang in the air for a moment, plummeted like a cannonball, then landed in a roll before springing to his feet.

"Okay, that was cool!" If Elias grinned any wider, Nyree thought, his teeth might fall out.

"Wow," whispered Faltha, reverently, "Brother!"

"Nope. Her brother though," said Elias, pointing at Nyree. "Who are you?"

"Elias, this is Faltha." Nyree pulled herself together

as the adrenaline burst ebbed away. "She's the emissary of the Seelie Court. Don't worry, I'll catch you up on the details later."

"Well then, hi Faltha of the Seelie Court." Elias gave a quick bow, not sure how else to greet a court emissary. "Seriously, though, why did you call me brother?"

"She called you brother," Malachite interjected, with something like disapproval in his voice, "because…"

"Because it's basically true!" Faltha interrupted. "He asked me gravel-head, so I'll do the answering, thank you."

Faltha turned back to Elias. "I called you brother because, like me, you are a being of magic. You see, your sister, it seems, is a sorcerer. She can shape magic to make things happen. You on the other hand, you are magic to your core. You don't shape it – you are the shape of it."

"See Malachite?" Elias said with a grin, "that's how to tell it! None of that 'manifestation' stuff. I really don't get how you can be so stuffy. I mean, how hard can it be to make *magic* a little magical?"

"Well, as you have it so well in hand," rumbled Malachite, turning away, "I expect you won't be needing me anymore." Malachite strode off, his footsteps falling heavy as gravestones on the hillside.

"Elias! How dare you talk to Malachite that way?" Nyree flushed red with fury, even as Elias's skin started to lose its blue tinge. "Malachite is only trying to help us. Don't forget, your leaping and capering just now was his idea. Really… Urgh! Boys!" With that Nyree stormed off after Malachite.

"Huh." Elias shrugged. "Wonder what got under her

skin. I only meant that you said it nicer."

"Of course I did. I'm a faery of the Seelie Court. Beauty is what we do." Faltha flitted around Elias, inspecting him from every angle. "Speaking of which... one moment!" Faltha darted off to the tree line and grabbed a drifting thistle seed.

"Faltha? Are you alright?"

"Shush, I'm listening!" After a moment, she fluttered back over. "Ah well, another one for the new-tech pile. Anyway, where was I?"

"You were about to tell me about the Seelie Court?"

"Right, yes so I was. The Seelie Court..." Faltha was concentrating so hard on getting her train of thought back on the rails she nearly stopped flapping her wings. "Yes! Your little aerobatics display. It got me thinking. Once you're in full control of your powers I think you would go far in the Seelie Court. You could even be a prince one day."

The briefest flicker of a smile on Elias's face showed that the flattery had hit home. However, he had more important things on his mind. "You mean that I will be able to control this?"

"Sure you will. It's just like walking and talking. It takes a bit of time, that's all. A bit of practice."

"But Malachite said..."

"Ah, Malachite!" Faltha sighed theatrically, "Well, he's just a construct really. He was made by a wizard to serve a purpose. He's not really a faery being like us."

"You say 'us' like we're the same. But I was made too. Surely, I'm more like Malachite, aren't I?" Elias looked over his shoulder, the way Malachite had gone, wishing that he'd made a bit more effort to be polite.

"Silly boy!" Faltha chuckled infuriatingly. "First of all, you were a person before you were changed. Malachite was just a pile of rocks before the wizard gave him form and life. You're nothing like Malachite. Anyway, you don't really think that all faery folk are born that way, do you?"

Elias nodded slightly, "Well, I hadn't really thought about it to be honest."

"Well, take vampires for example." Faltha perched on a crumbling stump of wall. "Pretty much all of them were human at some point."

"So, I'm like a vampire then?" Elias shuddered, blue fringing his face slightly. "You're quite sure that's the example you're going with?"

"Werewolves then?" Faltha tried.

"Not helping!"

"Oh-oh-oh, I know!" Faltha shot to her feet in excitement, "Who you're most like is the Great Imp!"

"The great imp?" asked Elias.

"Well, legend has it that centuries ago there was a boy so full of life and splendour and beautiful mischief that Nimueh, our queen, gave of her own essence to make him one of us." Faltha settled back down, knees drawn up, wings flickering rapidly behind her. "Now there was a faery! Such a sense of humour! You know the Loch Ness Monster?"

"Um, yeah." Elias's head was slightly spinning from the apparent change of subject.

"His work!"

"What do you mean his work? He made the monster?" Elias was totally lost now.

"No. It was a fake. A hoax. A beautiful joke!" Faltha was beaming now, her wings fanning so fast she almost took off. "And the most perfect thing about it was people started believing in magic just a little more! Genius."

"That's the most brilliant thing ever." Elias was grinning now too. "So really you think I'm a bit like him?"

"Oh, more than a bit my dear, right down to the beautiful blue skin." Faltha gave him an appraising look, "Yes, I really do think you will go far…"

54

Chapter 6

Sorcery

Nyree caught up with Malachite at the tower's garden. Among all the ruins this part alone looked almost maintained. Malachite's sanctuary of order amid a chaotic world.

"Malachite! Wait!" Nyree called, "I'm sure Elias didn't mean it. He's a wee toe rag sometimes and has about as much tact as a brick." She winced at the unintended rock pun.

"No, he didn't mean it badly." Malachite still faced away. "He has a good soul. I can see that. The magic wouldn't have chosen him otherwise. He may not be entirely wrong either. I don't know how much I can teach him about his condition. Faltha does, in fact, understand better what he's going through. I'm not well equipped to train a new faery. I was supposed to tutor a wizard in sorcery and spell craft. That's how I was made. The wild magic of faery kind is quite simply beyond me."

"Well, being right doesn't excuse being rude." Nyree scowled at the memory of her brother's flippant cruelty. Something Malachite had said snagged her attention. "Sorcery and spell craft? Is there a difference?"

"Well, yes!" Malachite straightened as he spoke. A little confidence showed in his voice. "Sorcery is raw power tamed by will. Spell craft is the subtle art of combining those sorcerous powers to create more complex results."

"Like drawing?" Nyree asked, a thoughtful look on her face.

"Explain?" A hopeful warmth filled that one-word.

"Well, it's pretty straight forward to just put pencil to paper and start sketching," said Nyree. "You can draw some pretty cool things that way. But eventually you want to draw something complicated. It's easier to think of those as lots of simpler shapes all blended together. That way, you can practice the simpler shapes and get good at them. Then when you need to you can build up a picture of anything you need… Something like that?"

Malachite beamed. "Exactly!"

"We'll start with sorcery, then?"

"A very good place to start." Malachite smiled widely as he went on. "While being by far the simpler of the magical crafts, it is the hardest to learn to do well. Indeed, many magic-wielders managed only the most rudimentary sorcery, trusting instead to spell-craft to do their will. At its heart sorcery is no more than simply forming an idea in your mind." Malachite held out one open hand, palm up. "Then, by summoning power to that idea it becomes real."

As he spoke a bright ball of light burst into being just above his hand. "The more finely you can focus your concentration," he closed his eyes, brows furrowing in effort, "the better the result you can achieve." As Malachite's eyes reopened the ball turned into a glowing flower.

"Amazing…" Nyree breathed.

Malachite let out a deep sigh, lowered his hand and the light-flower blinked out. "Most practitioners can only manage the simplest of conjurings. However, at least the fundamentals are needed before we can advance to spell craft."

"Okay," said Nyree in a hushed tone, "so where do I start?"

"Well, summoning a little light seems to be a good simple beginning." Malachite held out his hand again, nodding for Nyree to copy. "Now, imagine a ball of light filling your hand."

"Okay." Nyree nodded. "Got it."

"Now comes the tricky part," Malachite said softly as a slumbering lion. "Find the power within you and make it real."

Several moments passed and nothing happened. "Alright, so… not got it, then." Nyree sat down heavily on a low stone wall.

"Patience, my dear. Have another try."

Nyree gritted her teeth, nodded sharply, and tried again. Still nothing happened. Finally, she reached the end of her patience. Nyree stamped her foot, threw open her hand and yelled, "Just work okay!"

Warmth filled her chest like a gulp of too-hot soup. The burning shot down her arm raking its heat along her nerves. Light blazed from her hand, so bright she could have seen it through closed eyelids.

"Well done!" Malachite shouted triumphantly. Then his mask of composure snapped back on and his voice lowered. "Now, try it again. Without the dramatics, this time, if you can manage, please."

Nyree hesitated before complying. After the initial shock of sensation, the flow of magical energy made her feel more alive and more real than ever before. She closed her hand slowly and felt the magic trickle and die. As if trying to trick the magic into staying she snapped her hand open again.

Nothing. Not even the faintest glow. Her body felt empty. As useless as a rock. Nyree sighed and bowed her head in defeat. Without that enervating thrill she felt as inert as butchered meat.

"No," said Malachite, "don't give up. You need to remember how you felt when it worked."

Nyree knew he was trying to help. But remembering how success felt made it worse. What if she couldn't do it again? What if that was the last time she ever felt that thrill? Was this her lot? Peaked at eleven.

Malachite lay his huge stone hand on Nyree's shoulder. She thought it was supposed to be comforting but it vaguely squashed her. Malachite snatched his hand back as if burned.

"Remember the feeling just before you managed and call upon that again."

That wasn't a problem. Resolve took over Nyree's face as she remembered the frustration of her previous failures. She drew on her fury at struggling with this simple magic. Her fear of disappointing everyone crept in, unbidden. Under that mess of feelings, she felt a flutter of something different, something magical. In her mind, Nyree grasped the magic and let everything else fall away. The warmth built in her chest again. Now there was no fear, no fury, just the living thrum of magical power. She let it run, a slow trickle down her arm, and revelled in the feeling. A gentle light shone from her hand, pure and white.

"Well done." Malachite nodded, pride glowing on his rocky face.

The following hours passed dream-like in a flurry of the wildly improbable. Under Malachite's guidance, Nyree quickly learned how to create fire and move rocks around. Shaping the magic was as easy as following a flight of fancy. Controlling the water in the stream proved an interesting challenge for a while, but before too long Nyree was able to squirt small fish through floating rings of water. That had surprised Malachite, who muttered something about a 'prodigious imagination' and 'being a very promising sign'.

In the afternoon, Malachite set Nyree a control exercise. He gave her small trellises of foraged sticks. Nyree's task was to train roses to grow up them, using tiny bursts of magic to make buds grow in the desired direction. After fourteen bushes, Nyree felt that she had the hang of this task.

"So, what next Malachite?" she asked enthusiastically.

"What do you mean?" asked Malachite in return. "They're not done yet. I see ten more still to work on."

"Oh," Nyree tried not to show her disappointment. After all she was learning magic. Still. "I'd just hoped to try something new."

Malachite smiled gently at her. "The trick to really learning something is not to practice it until you get it right, but instead to practice until you can't get it wrong."

Nyree straightened slightly. He was right, of course. There was no point only part-learning something wonderful. She scoured the remaining bushes with a look of determination and turned back to her task.

The familiarity of the assignment allowed Nyree's mind to wander. A flock of starlings caught her eye as they wheeled through the air as if in a mass dance. Another rose trained. She moved on. There, by the next bush, she spotted a robin, hopping about on the ground.

"Watch what you're doing," rumbled gently over the garden to her.

"Sorry," mumbled Nyree. She dragged her attention back to the roses. Another one trained. Slightly wobbly in places, she noticed. *Malachite probably has a point,* she mused. *There's that robin again, oh look – it's flying off. I wonder what it would be like to fly.*

"Nyree, that is very impressive," called Malachite, "but would you please pay attention to the job in hand."

"What?" Nyree looked around to see what Malachite

was complaining about. Then she looked down. "Oh! Cool!"

Malachite was complaining that, instead of growing roses in pretty patterns, Nyree was hovering a metre above the ground.

"Yes, very 'cool', now will you please come down. Flying is very advanced sorcery. I don't think we should be exploring it today."

With a groan of disappointment Nyree sank back to the ground. "It was cool though," she said softly as she returned to her practice with the roses.

Malachite watched her thoughtfully for a few more moments, a smile playing over his lips. "You know, I do think that you are good enough with the roses for the time being. Shall we move on to something a bit different?"

Nyree finished growing the rose bush she was working on, then turned to Malachite. "Okay, I'm ready. What are we going to try now?"

"Well, if we are extremely careful, I think that we can experiment with that flying invocation you were just using."

"Really!" Nyree shouted in her excitement. She could feel the warm power building again and let it. She channelled the energy slowly and gently. Her feet lifted off the ground.

"Indeed," rumbled Malachite. "Carefully, now. I have never flown, myself. I rather think that I'm not at all built for it."

"Thank you, Malachite," crowed Nyree. "This is amazing!"

"Now, slowly will yourself forward. You might find that leaning into your movements will help focus your thoughts."

Nyree leaned forward and, shakily at first, started to move. By the time she had passed the garden wall, Nyree was getting to grips with how to move through the air. Still moving slowly, she tried a few gentle turns. When those worked out well, she climbed a little higher.

"Okay, very good," called Malachite from the garden. "Now, a little more speed but don't get carried away. And stay nearby. I can't help you if you fly too far away."

Nyree nodded. Even that small lapse of attention made her wobble in the air. A flash of fear was nearly her undoing, but Nyree pulled herself together and regained control. Gently, gradually she willed herself to go faster. Her brisk walking pace slid through to a quick jog and on to a frantic dash. She turned her face into the wind and felt it pull her hair back, wild and free. The magic soared through her. This was real. This was true. This was how she was meant to be.

She flew in a wide circle around the garden. On the second lap Nyree tried a few little swoops. The roller-coaster thrill led her higher and higher until she was well above Malachite's reach. After two more laps, Nyree was managing rolls and corkscrews along her path.

"Excellent," Malachite shouted up. "Now, I'd like you to come back down so we can plan our next step."

"Could I just try one more thing first?"

"Very quickly then, one last thing."

"I want to see how fast I can go." Nyree shot off over

the forest, screaming an excited whoop as she went.

"What was that?" asked Elias as he raced into the garden with Faltha close behind.

"That was your sister," scowled Malachite without taking his eyes off the quickly departing Nyree, "doing something incredibly foolish."

"Aw, and she didn't even invite me!" Elias pretended to sulk but couldn't quite wipe the grin off his face.

"I'm sure we can come up with plenty of trouble ourselves," offered Faltha, who looked slightly less enthusiastic than Elias.

"We don't need trouble," growled Malachite, his eyes still on the treeline. "We need these two to get to grips with their new powers *before* there's trouble."

Nyree came rocketing back and stopped abruptly above the garden. "Elias! Look what I can do!"

The magic fled like mice from a cat as Nyree's attention shifted to sharing her news. She yelped and tumbled from the air.

The entire garden exploded with activity. Elias leaped up to try to catch her. Malachite shot out a burst of magic toward Nyree. Faltha fluttered back out of the way. Malachite's magic, intended to slow Nyree's fall, instead hit Elias as he jumped into its path. His jump slowed to a stand -still. There was no way he'd reach her in time.

Nyree sent out a panicked blast of magic making the grass and moss under her erupt with growth. Nyree landed and sank deep into the overgrown foliage before springing gently back up.

"Knew you could do it," breathed Faltha.

"That was close." Nyree giggled nervously.

It took an hour for Elias to get back to the ground. The whole time, it felt like he was moving through custard. Every movement was smooth and easy if he went slowly, but otherwise it was like pushing against a wall. When he finally landed, Elias was seething, and very blue.

Malachite had apologised, of course, in his pompous, overly formal way. He probably even meant it. Didn't stick around for the spell to wear off though, just called out that the magic would finish by the time he hit the ground. Faltha stuck by him throughout, which was a relief. She'd told tales of the glory days of the faery courts, including a first-hand account of Janet and Tamlin's story. That had been an eye opener.

"So, when are you going to show me faery magic?" he asked Faltha as soon as he could.

"Faery magic?" said Faltha, confused for a moment, "Oh, sorry, we don't really do magic. At least not the sorcery rubbish that stone-head over there does."

"Oh," said Elias, disappointedly sinking onto Nyree's mound of moss. "Huh, this really is quite comfortable."

"All that nonsense is just so inelegant," she went on. "Nothing like our wonderful Glamour."

"Glamour?"

"Yeah, the magic of believing!" Faltha fluttered her wings in excitement. "With sorcery, you can make things happen, sure, but that doesn't make anyone believe it.

Glamour is the opposite. Nothing actually changes except everyone's belief."

"But what good is that?" sighed Elias. "Surely making stuff happen is way more powerful than just making people think something's happening."

"Really? What an amazing notion." In her surprise, her wings paused in their beating. "Completely wrong of course. Belief is what makes the world go around."

"Easy to say, but I don't believe…" Elias raised an eyebrow, thinking about what he was about to say. "Go on, please," he prompted instead.

"Well, take Nessie as an example. If she were real but nobody believed in her, how many research trips do you think would happen?"

"Fair point." Elias saw where Faltha was going.

"And how many tourists would visit hoping for a sighting?" pressed Faltha.

"I guess, basically none."

"The Loch Ness Monster is, in fact, one of the most powerful Glamours ever cast." Faltha's wings were now a blur of motion. "Truth be told we don't know how The Great Imp did it. Direct Glamours like that usually fade in a few days, he must have done something special to make it last for years like it has. Sure, the term 'Loch Ness Monster' has only been with us since 1933, but sightings go back to 565AD! I mean, fifteen hundred years. Now tell me that hasn't changed the world."

"Okay, I see what you mean." Elias remembered his sister flying. "Flying would be cool though," he said wistfully. "Believing I'm flying kind of isn't the same."

"Well, that's fair, I suppose," said Faltha, "but you still believe that I'm right in front of you talking, when in fact," she suddenly disappeared, only to reappear instantly behind Elias, "I've been over here since I started telling you about Nessie."

"Wow!" shouted Elias, "Did you just teleport?"

"No, silly, I just made you believe that I was over there," said Faltha, "while I moved around here. You didn't see me move because you believed that I wasn't moving."

"Okay," breathed Elias. "Now that I can use."

"See? I mean, sure, it's tricky to do practical things, but that's why it's beautiful."

"I am concentrating!" yelled Nyree furiously.

"Concentrating! You're not even looking," growled Malachite. "Nyree," he continued more gently, "it's important that you learn this. You have a great deal of power within you. Your imagination, your ability to create wonders in your mind, could make you one of the most powerful sorcerers that ever lived. However, it will all be for nothing if you can't learn to focus your attention. Worse, if you don't concentrate, you could end up hurting yourself and your brother."

"Are you sure he'll be alright?" Nyree glanced nervously toward the garden for the hundredth time since they had left Elias hanging in mid-air.

"Yes, he's fine. I expect he'll be a bit cross once the magic wears off." said Malachite "That is part of the reason why we're giving him some space just now. The rest of the reason is so that we can do some meditation exercises and hopefully teach you to concentrate so that we can avoid a repeat of that episode. Now, please return to the ground and try again."

Glancing down, Nyree realised that she was once again floating gently above the ground. She lowered herself to sit cross-legged on the grass, growling at herself in frustration. She closed her eyes, resolved to do better, and conjured a small yellow light.

"Good," said Malachite, walking steadily around her in a circle. "Now stay calm and concentrate on keeping the light steady."

Suddenly, Malachite slammed his hands together in a thunderous clap like the collapse of masonry. Just as suddenly Nyree's steady light turned into a blazing fireball which shot out toward the sound. A ring of shields sprang out of the ground surrounding Nyree.

"Sorry, sorry. I totally lost it there." Nyree removed the shields with a wave of her hand. "That really startled me though."

"Don't worry," said Malachite, "it takes more than a little fire to harm me."

Malachite sat next to her on the grass. "You know I wonder if we are approaching the issue incorrectly."

"Really? How so?"

"Well, we are fighting against your natural instincts. You are by nature curious. Given to drifting from one flight of fancy to the next. This might not be a bad thing in itself. As we've just seen, you are able to respond both quickly and creatively to the unexpected. With experience, I think that those responses will become more appropriate. I wonder if perhaps, rather than trying to constrain your creativity, we should learn to channel it more effectively."

"Sounds good, but why the sudden change?" asked Nyree.

"Well, as I said to Elias, I'm new to teaching. Indeed, I have never actually learned magic myself."

"What? But you…"

"My master created me with a working understanding of sorcery. Every trait that my master thought I would need was included from the outset. The point is…" Malachite lowered his face into his hand and rubbed his forehead, as if trying to dispel a headache. "The point is, that I have no experience of learning the basic principles of magic."

Nyree leaned over against his stony shoulder. She tried to put an arm around him, although she could barely reach across his back.

"I think you're doing okay," she said softly.

"For fifteen hundred years I have searched for the tools to help you in the battles to come. How can I have been so blind to the simple truth of training a wizard from nothing?" He sighed and turned toward Nyree. "Thus far, I have been attempting to form you as a sorcerer in my own image. All I know of magic are the rules and strict focus of an ancient stone man. It is clear to me now that that is not your way. We must find another."

"Okay, so what now, then?"

"My error, I think has been in trying to improve your sorcery by addressing your main flaw."

Nyree nodded, considering his words carefully until a bird flitted past. Elias had mentioned that Malachite had spoken to a chiffchaff that morning. She found herself wondering whether all birds spoke the same language. She turned to ask Malachite and found her teacher smiling patiently at her. "Sorry, Malachite. You were saying?"

"Clearly, your concentration is not something that we are going to improve easily by direct effort."

Malachite leaned his chin heavily on his hand. His elbow rested on his knee, and Nyree was struck by how much he looked like that famous statue she'd seen in France with her grandmother. She opened her mouth to comment, then thought about what Malachite was saying. She closed her mouth again with a snap.

After a moment, Malachite continued. "At any rate, I think that we should focus on your strengths instead as a way to avoid your weakness altogether."

"How do we do that?" muttered Nyree.

"Enchantments." Malachite looked as if this explained everything.

"And enchantments are?" Nyree waited hopefully.

"The imbuing of an object with a specific magical intention. In essence, the object then provides the shape of a spell, into which vessel you then deliver the power." Malachite looked around as if searching for something. "So first we need an object." His gaze fell on a fallen oak branch, "Ah, that will do nicely, I think. Summon it, please."

Nyree held out her hand and let out a little burst of magic. The branch stood up, then danced over toward them. Malachite rolled his eyes theatrically but smiled nonetheless.

Once the branch arrived in Nyree's hand Malachite began the lesson. "The main skill in enchantment is to form the magical idea in your mind without adding any power. Most sorcerers struggle at this point. There is an instinct to power the magic, which would cast it immediately and thus the enchantment itself would fail. Now, hold in your mind the same idea you had when you flew."

Nyree concentrated for a moment, then ever so slightly lifted off the ground. "Ah, sorry..." her frown deepened, and she dropped back down and stayed there. "Right, got it."

"Okay," said Malachite gently, "now push the idea into the branch."

Through her frown, one eyebrow lifted slightly then fell again. "Oh, I felt it go," she whispered.

"Alright then," said Malachite, barely whispering now, himself, "now call to mind an image of it being sealed in. Power *that* idea."

"Done."

"And relax," said Malachite, his voice returning to normal. "So that was, in theory, your first enchantment. Shall we see if it worked?"

"Alright," said Nyree straightening up. "What do I do?"

"Just push some unformed power into the branch. The enchantment will do the rest."

Nyree held the branch close. She reached for the

magic, surprised at how quickly that was becoming an easy habit, and pushed some into the branch. She shot into the air.

Malachite called up to her: "As long as you push power into it, you'll keep flying."

Nyree flew around the tower to the garden, where she saw that Elias was moving at a normal speed again. She swooped down, grabbed his hand, and flew off again. Elias's yelp of surprise turned quickly into a hoot of joy as he realised what was happening. They skimmed over the treetops with Elias's feet whipping through the topmost leaves.

"You okay down there?" yelled Nyree over the rushing wind.

"This is so cool!" replied Elias grinning widely.

"Hang on!" Nyree shouted, "I've always wanted to do this!"

They shot straight up into the air, climbing higher and higher before finally bursting through a cloud. They hovered, hanging perfectly above a rolling cotton-wool cloudscape.

"That was amazing!" panted Elias, a blue sheen of excitement rippling over his skin. "Are you sure we're safe though? You remember what happened last time."

"Yeah." Nyree grinned nonchalantly. "I've enchanted this branch, so I don't need to concentrate to maintain the magic."

"Awesome! So, it's completely under control then?" Elias smiled wickedly.

"Yup," Nyree grinned. "Completely under control."

"Well then…" Mischief danced on Elias's face. He let go and plummeted straight down.

"Elias!" Nyree screamed.

She flipped over and flew after him as fast as she could. Through the clouds with eye-watering speed. She spotted him dropping quickly below her. The wind tore at her face, ripped at her t-shirt. She pushed on faster and faster. Desperation drove her on. It was working. The gap closed. The trees rushed closer. Nyree reached out her free hand to catch her brother. Her fingers closed on his wrist. Elias vanished.

There was a familiar cackle of demonic glee next to her ear. Glancing around, Nyree saw Elias clinging on to her shoulders.

"That was brilliant," chortled Elias. "The look on your face!"

"What were you thinking!" screamed Nyree swatting at him with her free hand. "I almost had a heart attack. What on earth was that."

"Just a bit of faery glamour." Elias grinned. "Faltha said I should practice whenever I got the chance. I thought of it while we were up there and just couldn't resist. Sorry." His impish grin suggested he wasn't *very* sorry.

"Okay, back to the tower for us," sighed Nyree. Her grip on the branch trembled. "I think that's enough excitement for now."

Chapter 7

Spell-craft and Deceit

When Elias and Nyree arrived at the tower the next morning they saw Malachite and Faltha engaged deeply in a hushed conversation. Seizing the chance, Elias grabbed Nyree's sleeve and made a shushing sign. After a moment of concentration and a very brief flicker of azure skin, he vanished leaving Nyree just inside the gateway of the crumbling outer wall.

Nyree sighed and slipped back out to hide behind the wall. Tension briefly flickered across her forehead and she held in her mind the idea of seeing through Elias's eyes. This was tricky. Imagining actual objects, or physical changes in the world was easy, but abstract ideas like this were much harder. Nyree unleashed a brief puff of power and her whole world lurched. She smiled as she realised that she was seeing through Elias's eyes. Her joy was drowned by a wave of nausea as her viewpoint rolled about unpredictably.

"What are you doing Elias?" she whispered, leaning against the wall for stability. She closed her eyes against the dizzying sight. Then she realised – her brain couldn't predict how Elias was moving. This was just like getting seasick. An idea took her. She shut her eyes against the pitching vision. Nyree held onto the idea of Elias's sight, and reached for his other senses. It was an odd concept to frame in her mind. Certainly, it wasn't normal, visual imagining. On the other hand, the two ideas fitted together well, once Nyree had captured them both. Magic flowed into the new construct and Nyree lost herself completely.

It wasn't like she was inhabiting Elias, as a person distinct from herself. For all relevant purposes, she *was* him. Nyree could vaguely sense her own body, still standing by the wall, but only as an irritating distraction. At least the nausea had gone.

Elias clambered up the tower wall and settled on a doorway arch just above Malachite.

"I fear to stretch them too far too soon," said Malachite.

"I don't think you're giving them enough credit," Faltha shot back. "Anyway, it's necessary. People have started to notice already. Mostly faery folk, but not entirely. The court has a team out glamouring forgetfulness into the humans who have seen us."

"I had imagined your court would be thrilled," Malachite grumbled, "what with the extra belief in magic and so forth."

"Don't be such a block-head," Faltha replied acidly. "A bit more believing in magic is fine, but we don't want full scale investigations. You know that. Besides," she added, "it's not just human notice we might want to avoid. Not all is well in the faery world. There are rumours that the Red Caps are meeting again in secret. Bands of faeries are going rogue, turning from their Courts as if their vows meant nothing. Mostly from the Unseelies, of course, but even the Seelie Court has had some rebels. A month ago, I heard a rumour that a Grand Coven of witches would meet soon. Something's up. I don't think we should be advertising that the Tower is open for business again."

"Irrespective of your flighty gossip, the necessity of the action is irrelevant," Malachite sounded irritated. "I don't think it's time to introduce such advanced magic to the children. You and I can do it. We would be sure of success and as you say it needs to be done."

"And miss an opportunity like this? What kind of teacher are you?" said Faltha with an undisguised sneer in her voice.

"I worry that a failure would hurt them… set them back."

"You fear that they will surpass you!"

"I…" Malachite trailed off in a sigh, slumping with the sound of a closing tomb. "Very well, they will try."

Elias had been meaning to jump out, interrupt them at a suitably awkward moment, but in the end he slipped away silently to re-join Nyree at the outer wall. He didn't know what that was all about. He was pleased with Faltha's confidence, but he didn't like that she spoke to Malachite like he was a naughty school-boy.

When he reached Nyree the two nodded to each other in silent agreement. They launched into a raucous caper as they wandered up through the gateway, laughing and joking just like the schoolkids they were.

As they reached the tower Nyree called out, "What are we up to today, Malachite?"

"Ah, Nyree, Elias." Malachite's words carried an edge of tension. "Good morning! Today we shall attempt something rather advanced. Quite grand, actually. Now don't worry if it doesn't entirely go according to plan, but Faltha and I think that you both have a good chance of success."

"Yeah, strong opening stone-man!" needled Faltha. "Elias, you've got this kid. If your spell-weaving sister can deliver, then we're golden."

"Thank you, Faltha," Malachite said through gritted teeth.

"Okay, so what actually is it we're to do?" Nyree spoke carefully. She didn't want to let on that they'd been eavesdropping. Apparently, Malachite's worry was infectious. Nyree could feel her shoulders tugging at her neck. She shrugged to loosen them.

"Ah, yes. Well," said Malachite, "today we are going to attempt," he glanced at Faltha, as if daring her to interrupt, "to cloak the tower."

"Cloak the tower?" Elias's wide eyes underlined the note of panic in his voice. "The whole tower?"

"Well, yes actually. People have already started

noticing goings on around here." Malachite responded matter-of-factly, "Faltha and I both feel that it would be best if we avoided attention for the time being."

"Okay," gulped Elias, "but the whole tower? You don't think that we could start smaller?"

Malachite drew a breath to respond, but Nyree cut in. "Of course, Malachite's lesson plan starts us off with something smaller. He's letting us know what we can achieve by the end of the day if we pay attention. Dope."

Malachite nodded curtly. Nyree thought she saw a flicker of relief around his eyes.

"Alright then, Elias," said Malachite drawing himself up. "I'm sure Faltha has taught you, by now, how to disappear?"

Elias grinned then obligingly vanished. He re-appeared and theatrically bowed, point proven.

"Good, now using the same technique can you make this stone disappear?" Malachite gestured to a boulder, long ago fallen from the tower wall.

"Uh, I don't know," said Elias frowning at the rock furiously, "I'll try."

His face set with grim determination, Elias stared at the rock and vanished. He reappeared a second later muttering to himself. If scowls were deadly the rock would have crumbled to dust. Still nothing happened.

Elias's skin started shifting through sapphire, gradually deepening into the furious darkness of a twilight storm. Finally, with a grunt Elias stopped. Defeated. By a rock.

"Yeah, not really the same technique at all," put in

Faltha. "When you make yourself invisible you…"

"Imagine myself invisible, then believe it's so," recited Elias.

"With other things it's different. You have to project. Imagine you are the rock."

"Imagine I'm the rock?" Elias wasn't sure he'd heard right.

"Yeah, just pretend that you're a dull grey blob on the landscape, not really doing anything worthwhile." Faltha glanced witheringly at Malachite. "If you were a person, you'd be stupid and useless. Got it?"

"Sort of…"

"Good, now just imagine that you aren't there at all," Faltha chirped. "Then believe in it and whoosh: vanished rock."

"Okay. So, kind of similar." Elias nodded. The rock faded, like it wasn't sure what it was supposed to do, then vanished.

Faltha glowered at Malachite, her wings flickering in agitation. She turned back to Elias wearing a smile of sunshine and daisies. "Perfect, good job. Now hold that for a moment, it's your sister's turn."

"Yes." Malachite stepped aside pointing to where the rock was. "Nyree, hold your hand over the stone, and try to feel Elias's glamour."

Nyree stepped over and, as she held out her hand, felt the slightest tingle. She would have missed it if she hadn't been expecting it.

"Interesting," she murmured. "It feels like telling Dad I was doing homework when I was really making him a

78

birthday present."

"Very good, Nyree," said Malachite, smiling as if all his hundreds of birthdays had come at once. "Faery magic often has the feeling of unrepentant dishonesty. Very good, indeed. Now, do you remember how you sealed the flying magic into the branch yesterday?"

"Mmm hmm." She frowned. The tickly lying feeling kept sneaking away while she tried to focus on Malachite's words.

"Well, this is just the same." Malachite smiled at Faltha. "Seal the deceit into the stone."

The memory of enchantments and the feel of the glamour both slipped in and out of her mind. Each one vying for the top spot in her attention. When the two thoughts coincided a third part of her mind pounced with the magical power to enact the sorcery. A fourth part boggled at the juggling act of the other three, then smirked wryly at itself.

"Done." Nyree sagged and swayed on the spot as she felt the magic take hold.

"Now, Elias," said Malachite, "you may relax."

"Huh, that's better." Elias dropped his glamour. The stone remained invisible.

"One problem though." Nyree didn't like to criticise. After all, she was rather proud of her work. But… "Can we turn it off? I'm definitely going to trip over this at some point."

"Don't worry, that's the easy part of the lesson." Malachite chuckled. "Elias, your skills aren't needed for this next part. I think you had best practice your cloaking glamour over by the gardens, while we work on this problem your sister has raised."

"Sure, Malachite." Elias turned to leave. "Faltha?"

Malachite turned to Nyree. "The next stage is going to take a bit of work on our part. This will be our first exercise in spell-craft. We need to add a second layer to the magic you've just performed. What you need to do is consider the first invocation. You do not need to do this in detail, thinking of the fact of it will suffice." He paused for Nyree to absorb this. "You then create the next layer in your mind. Once this is achieved, you carefully merge the ideas together, composing a spell. The spell is then powered with magical energy to be activated."

"Oh, you mean like this?" Nyree held out her hand. She summoned a ball of light. She poked the ball with her mind, shaping it to look like a bird. The bird flew off her hand and exploded in a shower of sparks. "Yeah, I thought of that this morning on the way here." She smiled hopefully at Malachite.

"Amazing." Malachite glowed with astonished pride. "You taught yourself the basics of spell-craft while on a walk in the woods. Incredible."

"Well," muttered Nyree, her cheeks reddening, "it just seemed like the thing to do."

"Amazing," repeated Malachite. "Anyway, time for the next layer of our cloaking spell. What we need is for people who already know where the rock is to see through the glamour."

Nyree added the next layer of magic and the rock duly reappeared. At Malachite's request Nyree closed her eyes. A few moments and a dull thud later, Malachite told her to open them again.

"The rock's gone." gasped a surprised Nyree.

"Only moved," responded Malachite. "Now that you don't know where it is, the glamour is hiding it from you again. However, if I stand on it like this," Malachite stepped up on to the suddenly visible again rock, "then your new layer of magic blocks the glamour allowing you to see it."

"Cool," grinned Nyree, "so this is what we're going to do to the whole tower?"

"That is indeed the plan," said Malachite. "However, first we need to unravel the magic and the glamour on this rock." Malachite shot a brief glance over to where Elias and Faltha were practicing, "We can't leave a stealth rock lying about for just anyone to move now can we?"

⊷⊙⊶

"Okay then, here goes!" Elias shot Nyree a weak smile, then turned back to the tower. He gritted his teeth and tried his glamour.

"No good," said Nyree, "you've missed the right side."

"Hmm," Elias huffed. "It isn't easy you know."

"I wasn't criticising. Just letting you know that you'd missed a spot." Nyree paused, then added, "If it helps, I can't make any of it disappear."

"You know, I think that does help." Elias held a deep breath then stared down the tower like he wanted it to blink first.

A tiny puff of magic zipped from Nyree's fingers and Malachite gave her a knowing smile. Elias felt his mind open up and wrap itself around the entire tower. He let the breath out in a slow steady hiss and the tower vanished from sight.

"Hold it just a moment," breathed Nyree rolling up her sleeves. She sent out power, the sealing magic already in her mind. "Okay, relax."

Elias let out the rest of the breath in a relieved sigh. "Didn't think I had that in me for a moment there."

"Good work," rumbled Malachite proudly, "now add the next layer please, Nyree."

"No rest…" mumbled Nyree. She released a burst of power. The tower flickered back into view.

"Right then," said Nyree. "Dinner time I think." Elias's belly rumbled right on queue. "See you tomorrow, Malachite!"

"Have a good one, Faltha," called Elias over his shoulder as they left.

◦◦⊰⊱◦◦

The next morning, Nyree strolled through the tower's outer gateway. Elias climbed over the tumble-down wall and leaped into the courtyard. He rolled through his landing, swept to his feet, and walked smoothly on like a cat with cream on its whiskers.

"Poser," said Nyree as she walked around him to the main door.

Within the broken walls of the tower stood Malachite, in front of what looked suspiciously like a sand-table.

"Good morning children," he called when he saw them. "Please approach so we can start today's exercises."

"After yesterday, I was hoping for something a little lighter," said Nyree, "but, I must admit, playing in a sand-pit isn't quite what I had in mind."

Malachite raised a craggy eyebrow. "I think you'll find this exercise quite challenging, in fact. We're going to use the sand for building models to redesign the tower. I think it is high time we built a place of learning worthy of its history. The infant's sand table is so that I don't have to bend so far."

"It's about time we set you up with something a bit less," Elias's gaze flicked around as he searched for the right word, "ruiny."

"Well, indeed. After nine hundred and seventy-three years of living in rubble waiting for you two to come along, I do think I may have earned some creature comforts."

"Quite right!" said Nyree, "Shall we get started?"

Elias hunted around, looking under the table, "Okay, where's the buckets and spades and stuff?"

"Oh, you won't be needing those. You are going to move the sand by magic," said Malachite. "Think of it as an exercise in control." He waved a hand over the sand. "Let us start with this." An intricate model of the tower ruins flowed up from the surface.

"Well, obviously," Nyree waved her hand in imitation of Malachite, "we'll want the outer wall repaired."

Mentally, she reached for the grains of sand and

began moving them one by one. An idea occurred to Nyree. It was magic, after all, why not ask for the impossible? She imagined an invisible chamber, exactly where she wanted, then pushed the sand into it all at once. The sand sprang up to form a high outer wall.

"Well done," smiled Malachite.

"And some side towers and buttresses to climb on and jump from!" Elias gestured excitedly at the sand, which didn't move. "Um... a little help?"

"No," said Malachite gently, "let us see how you choose to solve this problem yourself."

Elias paused for a moment, his head tipped slightly, one hand unconsciously cupping his chin. "Oh, I could do this!" He waved his hands dramatically and his skin flashed blue. A perfect miniature model of the desired features appeared around the broken-down sand tower.

"Wow!" Nyree gaped in surprise. Her outer wall collapsed as her attention switched to Elias's breath-taking model. "Oops, forgot to seal it." Moments later her wall was re-formed and fixed in place properly. Nyree leaned in to get a better look at Elias's additions. "How did you do that? You've even got the colours. Is that moss on those stones?"

"Well, I can't move the sand, obviously." Elias grinned. "So, I figured that I could just use a glamour to show what I wanted. It didn't make sense to make it look like a sand model when it could look like the real thing." He looked up at Malachite hopefully, "That's okay, isn't it?"

"Very impressive indeed." Malachite's rumbled tone was so warm that Elias blushed slightly.

Chapter 8

The Colours of Magic

The following days flew past. Nyree, Elias and Malachite became increasingly excited as their ideas poured out into the sand. By the end of the week, the designs were ready. From the astronomy deck at the top, down past the many minarets and buttresses, through to the basement storage.

"Well done children," said Malachite, "now that you have a good grasp of precision, it is time to start considering power. You are going to learn to turn your new abilities toward the brute-force process of building."

"I did wonder how we'd manage to get builders in for this," said Nyree. "Where do we start?"

"Nyree, your first task is to excavate the basement." Malachite turned to Elias. "You, Elias, will use your imp-strength to rebuild the outer wall."

"What's your job, Mal?" asked Elias, looking worriedly at the huge stones of the outer wall.

"Why, the hardest task of all." Malachite's stony face betrayed just a flicker of amusement. "Supervising you two."

Malachite waved his hand and created a comfortable chair formed out of the grass. A second gesture made small mounds of earth pull the planning table, sand models and all, into place next to him. Nyree shrugged and turned toward the tower, eyeing up the ground and considering the best way to go about digging with magic.

Elias turned toward the outer wall. Despite grumbling under his breath about child labour, he was keen to find out how strong he had become.

Nyree nodded to herself once and drew in a deep breath. She pictured the entire volume of earth where the basement was to go, held it in her mind and imagined it following her commands. She let out a careful trickle of power. Then, realising the enormity of the task ahead she released magic as fast as she could. Nyree raised her hands and a huge section of soil lifted. Nyree grinned triumphantly and raised the excavation clear above the ground.

"Very good," Malachite sounded as impressed as a schoolteacher in the last week of term. "Now where were you planning on putting it?"

"Oh," said Nyree, the smile falling from her face, "I hadn't thought of that." She let the earth slip back into its hole.

"The true art of magic," said Malachite, "is neither in how we focus power, nor how creatively we manifest it. The true art is in considering our actions and their consequences. In fact, the reason that the greatest of us are called wizards is the *wisdom* they apply in each of their works."

"Huh," Nyree sat down on the grass.

"Now don't give up…" began Malachite.

"Shhhh," said Nyree, "I'm trying to think."

Nyree held out her hand. Across the hillside her flying staff stood up and leaped into her grasp with a crisp smack. She lifted into the air until she had a good view of the whole site and hung in the air for a few moments before gently sliding to the ground. A calm smile glowed on her face. Nyree sank to one knee and pressed her fingers into the soft earth. She gasped as her fingers struck something hard. A twig? Summoning the magic, she drove her thoughts deep into the ground searching for what she needed. Found it. The images in her mind twisted like a flock of starlings.

The whole hilltop seethed as if it were boiling liquid. Huge stones, aged but cut into neat blocks, burst through the grass and marched along the hillside to arrange themselves in orderly stacks. At the same time, the soil within the tower flowed out underground to fill the gaps left by the massive stones. A few seconds after the improbable ballet of building materials started the sound of Dukas' 'Sorcerer's Apprentice' floated across the hill.

"Sorry," chuckled Elias from his seat on top of the outer wall, "couldn't resist!"

Elias dropped the massive block and jumped back growling a curse. He glared at his hands which were royal blue to his elbows.

Faltha fluttered near his shoulder, "What's the problem? You picked that up without so much as a blink."

"I can manage the weight," Elias sighed, "but every time I pick up the big ones my hands start to go blue."

"Are you surprised?" Faltha moved to perch on the stone in front of him. "The more you call on your magical nature, the more that nature shows itself."

"I'm just fed up with turning blue when I try to do the slightest thing."

"Slightest? Are you kidding?" Faltha sounded shocked, "That thing must weigh a couple of tonnes at least!"

"Ah, you know what I mean." Elias kicked the block in frustrated fury. Instead of the anticipated pain, his leg turned a brilliant blue and the boulder tumbled from its place. He dropped to his knees and covered his face with his hands.

"You don't want to turn blue?" Faltha looked stricken.

Had Elias shared his sister's powers, the look he threw at Faltha would have burned her to ashes. "Of course I don't want to turn blue!"

"Well, why on earth not?" yelled Faltha. "You look amazing! The princes of the faery courts themselves aren't so splendid."

"But I don't look human."

"No," said Faltha, more gently, "you don't. You're

88

more than that."

"I don't want to be more." Elias sounded defeated. "I just want to be me."

"This is you, now." Faltha gently touched his hand. "This is the real you."

"I know. It scares me though."

"It's a big change, and change can be scary sometimes. But," Faltha brightened, "it can bring some advantages too. Pick up that block again."

Elias stood and lifted the massive boulder. "Hey, I'm not blue this time!"

"I'm hiding it with a glamour." Faltha smiled weakly at Elias. "Now your turn."

Elias's arms flashed bright blue as Faltha's glamour dropped then blinked back to their normal colour as Elias took over. He grunted slightly, and the stone wobbled in his grasp.

"That got heavy."

"Yeah," said Faltha, "that's the problem. Your magic is like your attention. You can spread it about, or you can concentrate and do one thing really well. Like running while you're doing maths. You'll make mistakes, or you'll slow down, or you'll trip."

"Okay," said Elias, "this could work. I can do this."

Faltha sighed. "Yeah, you could."

"What's the problem?" asked Elias.

"Well," Faltha shook her head, "you're holding yourself back this way. Wasting your power on looking normal when you could be glorious."

"Are you kidding?" Elias glanced at the boulder in his

hands, easily the size of a sofa. "You think this isn't glorious?"

"It's impressive, sure," Faltha's wings flittered in agitation, "but you're holding yourself back, hiding your true self. You're pretending to be what you aren't, and to faeries that's about as un-beautiful as you get."

"Why'd you show me then?"

Faltha settled down slightly, "I was hoping to show you that hiding would just weaken you."

"I'm pretty sure I'm strong enough."

"Fine then," said Faltha flatly. "You go build your wall. I've got court business to see to."

Without another word Faltha flew off into the woods. Elias looked after her for a moment then with a shrug set to the task of rebuilding the tower's outer wall.

∞◦§◦∞

The days moved by in a pleasant monotony of magical construction.

Nyree used her sorcery to acquire resources salvaged from the wreckage of the original tower, as well as bringing materials in from the surrounding forest. Although Nyree could move things faster than Elias, placing them precisely with magic was so time consuming that it was better to have Elias assemble the stonework by hand. Nyree's magic then fused the stones together leaving an incredibly strong structure.

Disputes, while rare, occasionally arose. Mostly because Malachite wanted a comfortable and practical sorcerer's tower to live in, while Nyree and Elias hoped for something rather more adventurous.

Nyree scowled at the tower over her half-eaten sandwich.

"Whatever is the matter this time?" asked Malachite.

"Hmm?" Nyree looked up, "Nothing really, it's just..."

"Just what, my dear?"

"Well, it's just so grey." Nyree huffed, "Don't you think a splash of colour would be nice?"

"Well," said Malachite hesitantly, "that could be most pleasant, but colour magic tends to be a bit wayward."

"Okay," Nyree perked up. "Let's start small... How about that third-floor turret?"

Before Malachite could say anything to dissuade her, Nyree grabbed her flying stick and flew up.

A slightly strained "please be careful with my home!" floated up after her.

Nyree landed lightly on the balcony and stepped inside. She looked slowly around, a smile spreading on her face.

"Yes," she muttered, "let's get a little sunlight in here."

She summoned some magic and gathered the bright noon sunlight into a ball in the middle of the room.

"Now to add some colour..."

Nyree shaped her magic, rippling through the colour

spectrum trying out different shades. After a few cycles, she settled on a striking imperial purple. Nyree sent out a blast of power to fix the colour to the walls. Task complete, Nyree relaxed her mind and shut off the flow of magic. The colours blinked out.

"Oops." She pulled the spell back into her mind. The purple danced back onto the walls. Nyree drew her power again and, rather more forcefully, tried to fix the colours in place.

The sunshine ball wavered then detonated in a rainbow explosion, which threw Nyree back into the main body of the tower. She stood up rather shakily.

"What was that?" Elias yelled from the ground floor of the tower. Leaping up a floor at a time he shouted, "Are you alright?"

"Yeah, I'm fine." She was, largely. More than a bit shaken, though.

"Cool!" Elias landed on the banister railing opposite the turret door. Inside the turret looked like someone had placed an art shop in a spin dryer. Colours ran in a panic over every surface. Complementary colours seemed to flee each other, seeking out the company of the most violent clashes.

Malachite arrived on the landing. His mouth opened to speak. He saw the turret room and was stricken into stony silence.

"The look on your face!" Elias collapsed in a gale of laughter.

"Sorry, Malachite." Nyree had the decency to try to hold back the laughter.

"Well," managed Malachite at last, "I think this will prove a good venue for our lessons in spell-craft. May it serve to remind you of the dangers of rushing ahead."

Chapter 9

The Turret of the Winds

Nyree sat alone on the outer wall. She had rushed her breakfast and hurried out before Elias to grab a few moments on her own. She'd had an idea the night before and wanted to think it through in peace.

Elias leaped up and sat next to her. "You alright, sis?" he asked through a last mouthful of toast.

"I've had an idea." Nyree answered in a hushed tone. "Can you build me a turret room on its own? You know, not attached to anything."

"Why?"

"Trust me." Nyree grinned. "This is going to be awesome."

Elias shrugged and got to work. It turned out to be quite an unsettling experience. His recent building work had been precariously balanced on the outer face of the tower, which was getting quite tall. Taking extra care was, unusually for Elias, starting to become a habit. Although he was now building at ground level, Elias still found himself leaping from one support point to another, as if there wasn't just firm grass that he was avoiding in between.

Nyree was busily experimenting with a scale model that she'd hurriedly constructed. Her sketchbook was propped open beside her on a table made from a hastily summoned flagstone, the pages held down by a collection of small rocks.

The model clattered to the table once again. "Mm-hmm." Nyree rapidly jotted down some notes. "Right then. Next."

Every few minutes Elias would call over to Nyree, "Next one, sis!"

In response, Nyree would shoot magic over to the quickly forming turret, fusing the stonework in place.

They fell into a smooth rhythm, barely interrupting each other. After an hour, Malachite wandered over from his gardening on the far side of the half-formed tower.

"What are you two up to?" he asked, one craggy eyebrow twitching up in puzzlement.

"Experimental architecture," said Nyree, not looking up from her notes.

"Exactly how experimental, might I ask?" There was poorly hidden concern in Malachite's voice.

"Very careful experimental architecture," replied Nyree, who was not fooled in the slightest, "with diagrams, and maths and everything. I'm even rehearsing the spell work on a scale model. Please don't worry. It really is all under control."

"Well," Malachite turned to go back to his gardening,

"let's hope so, indeed."

Two hours later Elias was relaxing in the sunshine, slowly munching a packet of crisps. He savoured each one with a blissful expression on his face.

"You know," he said as he felt Nyree's shadow fall on him, "I think I might rush things a bit too much. It's nice taking the time to enjoy things sometimes."

"Hmm." Nyree scoffed. "Yeah, that'll last. I'm done experimenting. Ready to try it?"

"Cool! Yeah!" Elias devoured the remaining crisps in one impish mouthful. He glanced around for a bin and, not finding one, crammed the empty packet into his mouth as well.

"I wonder what happens to all that stuff," mused Nyree.

"Quit stalling," said Elias. "Let's do this."

Nyree sent a shimmer of magic to lift the new turret-room into the air. She manoeuvred it into position near the fifth floor of the tower. After taking a moment to compose herself, Nyree reached for more magic. She kept one hand pointing at the turret, holding it in place. The other, she twisted in a circular motion forming a whirlwind below the turret.

The gestures weren't strictly necessary. Malachite had scolded her repeatedly for her 'pointless hand-waving' but, as Nyree explained to him, it helped focus her mind on her task. Besides, Nyree felt it was simply more satisfying if you looked like you were doing magic rather than just standing very still while amazing stuff happened near-by.

Nyree lowered her arms, shaking out a slight ache. A

snap of her fingers and the spell was locked in place. She nodded in satisfaction at the morning's work.

"That," said Elias in a hushed tone, "is the most awesome thing I have ever seen."

A smile flickered over Nyree's lips. "Let's go check it out up close."

They ran up the hill to the tower, stopping just underneath the new turret. From below, the sight of the stonework held up just by whirling air, and a bit of dust for effect, was breath-taking.

"I really don't think this is a good idea," Malachite called as he came into view around the base of the tower. "In fact, I think you two would be well advised to step back quite far really rather quickly."

"Oh, spoil-sport," cried Nyree. "It's completely stable and entirely safe. I've been experimenting on this all morning to make sure I understand the system. Really, stop fussing and take a moment. It's quite something, isn't it?"

Just as Malachite took a breath to reply, a gust of wind blew through, gently bending the treetops. The airflow under the turret collapsed in chaotic spirals. Tonnes of masonry hung in the air for a stretched second before plummeting directly toward Nyree.

In her panic, Nyree flung up her arms but not her magic. Acting on instinct, Elias leaped clear. He landed. Glanced up to check that Nyree was safe. She wasn't. Glowing incandescent blue, he sprang back to rescue her.

He put everything into the effort. Faster than he'd ever moved before. Faster than a human eye could follow. Not fast enough.

Twisting in the air, he saw that he could get to Nyree, but couldn't get her clear in time. Too much rock. Far too close. Despair crashed down on him, as heavy as the turret. *Why hadn't he grabbed her as he'd leaped clear the first time?* The normally quiet voice of doubt now roaring through his thoughts. *How could he have just left her there? Stupid. So stupid.*

The despair turned to wild inspiration. As he landed, Elias grabbed Nyree. He shifted his weight and jumped straight up at the falling stone. Elias opened his mouth inhumanly wide and bit an enormous chunk of rock out of their path. They exploded up into fresh air, even as the turret disintegrated into rock-dust and rubble.

The pair landed hard on the ruins, still clinging to each other. Nyree was shaking and as white as a ghost. A low repetitive whimper escaped her throat. Elias, his skin fading now to deeper, cooler hues, gave a short laugh which quickly faltered. He tried to stand, wobbled, and thought better of it. His panic fuelled frenzy faded, leaving only exhaustion in its wake.

Chapter 10

Interlude

Elias stared at his breakfast with his knees drawn up to his chest. There was a sickly pallor to face as he pushed his spoon aimlessly around the bowl. His dad clattered around the kitchen, obliviously wittering about who knew what.

Elias dropped the spoon and curled up a little tighter for a moment. Grimacing, he let out a slow, hissing breath as the pain in his belly gradually eased off.

"Elias? Are you okay?" His dad's voice seemed to come from miles away.

"Yeah, Dad, I'm fine," mumbled Elias, taking deep, steadying breaths. "Just a belly-ache."

"Poor boy," said his dad ruffling his hair gently. "Too many sweets yesterday?"

"Something like that," groaned Elias.

"Good morning you two." Elias's mum bustled past and started rummaging for her favourite mug.

Dad smiled and finished pouring coffee into it before placing it on the table. "Like I'd make you hunt for things before your morning coffee."

"Oh, I love you." She said, wrapping herself around the coffee and taking a deep breath.

"Me or the coffee?"

"Yes," Mum said, smiling mischievously before adding, "dope."

"Now I really might be sick." Elias rolled his eyes.

Nyree shuffled into the room staring sightlessly ahead. Her hair was sticking out wildly and her nightie was on backwards. She assembled her breakfast without really looking, narrowly avoiding using orange juice instead of milk on her cornflakes.

"You alright sweetie?" asked her mum.

"Yeah," said Nyree in a distracted, not-really-there voice, "just didn't sleep well."

"Nightmares?" asked her dad.

"Yeah," Nyree mumbled around a mouthful of cereal, "just silly stuff though." She spotted her mum draw a breath and quickly added, "Nothing worth talking about."

After a few quiet moments, their mum asked brightly, "So, what shall we do today?"

"Aren't you going to work?" Elias frowned, putting his spoon back in his bowl.

"Work? Sweetie, it's Saturday."

"Oh, oops," Elias mumbled. "Lost track."

"Anyway," continued their mum, "I thought, if no one had anything else on, that we could go and explore

Aberdour castle this afternoon."

Nyree shuddered visibly and hunched down lower over her breakfast.

"What's the matter, my girl?" her dad looked concerned, "You usually love that sort of thing."

"Well, it's just… we just, that is…" Nyree looked desperately at Elias before continuing. "We were exploring some old ruins in the woods and a bit of wall fell off and nearly got me. Elias warned me in time, but it could have been nasty. Kind of freaked me out a bit I guess."

"Which is why you two need to be careful when you're out playing," said their dad, looking worried. "In fact, I think…"

"We're not," interrupted their mum, "going to ban you from exploring the woods. But we do need you to promise to be safer – a bit more sensible."

"Don't worry Mum," said Nyree, softly, "I don't want to go anywhere near those ruins again."

Elias looked up sharply, his face becoming even paler. "But we…"

"Now kids, you mustn't let fear control your choices," their mum began. At her husband's worried look she added, "Learn from it, sure. Don't go near the crumbling bits. Don't climb up high and certainly don't go under anything. Keep well away from everything that looks dangerous but that doesn't mean that you have to avoid the woods entirely. Okay?"

"Okay, Mum," said Nyree, weakly.

"Elias?"

"No problem. Keep off the high bits. Don't go under things. Be safe." Elias's face clenched up again and he added, "And don't eat too much junk."

They went to Aberdour that afternoon. A good solid lunch had left Elias feeling much better. For Nyree, the draw of an ancient castle and the sheer normality of a family outing outweighed her dread of more crumbling ruins.

The visit started pleasantly enough. A short walk through the pretty sea-side town led into the castle grounds. At first, the information plates about the thousand -year history of the buildings captured Nyree's attention. She was fascinated by the changing building techniques and how the style developed from fortress to luxury over the centuries.

In a darker area of the ruins, Nyree raised her hand ready to conjure some light. She stopped herself just in time – instead, reaching out to touch the wall. From behind her she heard a sound.

"Lumos," whispered a voice.

There was a burst of stark white light. Nyree spun around to see her dad grinning foolishly. His hand was raised high clutching his phone, its camera's flash shining brightly.

"Well," he said, "if you can't pretend to be a wizard in a place like this then there's really no helping you."

"So, we're pretending to be wizards?" Nyree pitched her voice to carry, "In that case, I think I hear some knights coming to steal our magic treasure."

Right on cue, Elias burst through the doorway, closely followed by their mum.

"Quick: stop them!" yelled Nyree, waving her hands at Elias and making a conscious effort *not* to stop him.

Dad spun around, torch in hand. He pointed it at Elias and drew a breath for another magic word. Without thinking Elias ducked, dived to the side, and rolled. He found his feet and started to flip off the wall. With an alarmed glance at Nyree, he twisted, let his feet slip from under him and landed with a thump on his backside.

"Well, that was much cooler in my head." He groaned, standing up with exaggerated slowness.

"Are you alright?" asked his dad.

"Yeah, I'm fine. Plus," Elias flashed a grin and made a grabbing motion at the air, "I've got your treasure!"

He slipped behind his mum, who drew an imaginary sword to cover him, and dashed for the exit.

Soon the whole family were cavorting around the ruins, roles and rules shifting fluidly from fantasy to fantasy. They finally arrived at the dovecot, which their Dad decided was a treasure hoard and he was the dragon guarding it. He roared and waved his arms wildly.

"Okay," grinned Nyree, "I think Dad maybe needs to have a cup of tea and some quiet time now."

"Oh, thank goodness," he said. "I'm not sure how much more I had in me."

"That was kind of weird, wasn't it?" said Nyree as she gazed out of her bedroom window at the two stars visible through the glare of streetlights.

"Just a bit," Elias was staring intently at the marble-run he was building. "I mean, a few weeks ago that would have been a cool place to play. It seemed daft though, running around an old castle playing make-believe when we've had a taste of the real thing."

"Well, that too," said Nyree. "What got me, though, was the number of times we almost reached out for magic. Without even thinking about it, really."

Nyree half turned, leaning her head back against the glass with a sigh. "It's like the world just isn't big enough now. Like, without magic all the colours are all shades of faded brown."

"What?" Elias looked up, raising an eyebrow. "The colours all look fine to me."

"No, I mean, everything seems a bit boring without magic." Nyree rolled her eyes. "Like today. We were strolling around the oldest standing castle in Scotland, and I kept thinking, Malachite could have watched this get built. It's suddenly just a bit less wonderful."

"Did you really mean it?" asked Elias, leaning back against the bed.

"Mean what?"

"When you said you didn't want to go back to the tower."

"I think so." Nyree leaned forward, drawing her knees up to her chest and hugging them. "I don't know. Maybe."

106

"You could actually leave it all behind? Never do magic again?"

"No," said Nyree, "I don't think I could. You?"

"Are you kidding?" Elias let his skin turn blue. "I can't really ignore this, can I."

"Sorry, Elias," Nyree straightened up and slid down from the windowsill to sit with her brother. "I didn't even stop to think. Of course, we'll go back. We have to."

"We have to," she repeated quietly to herself.

"I mean, thinking about it," Elias hid the blue on his skin, "things have only gone wrong when we stopped listening to Malachite."

"That's true."

"So, we need to learn about our powers, or we're going to hurt ourselves." Elias smiled now.

"Well, yeah…"

"So, in fact…" Elias grinned. "Going back is actually the best way to keep our promise to Mum and Dad to be safer."

"Imp," muttered Nyree, rolling her eyes.

Chapter 11

The Tower

The following morning there was a nervous tension over breakfast. Even their dad, who was usually quite oblivious to these things seemed to be picking up on it.

"What are you two planning to get up to today?" he asked, sipping at his tea.

"We thought that we might head back to the woods today." said Nyree. Her idea was that once she'd said it aloud, she would have to actually go rather than putting it off for another day.

"Okay," said Dad. "You're going to be safe, though. Right?"

Nyree's and Elias's nods were somewhat subdued. Their dad hastily plastered a wooden looking smile on his face and added, "Do you think a wizard once lived there?"

Nyree looked up sharply. Elias's breath caught in his throat. Then they saw the big, silly grin on their dad's face. They usually liked that he made the effort. A month ago, this would quite likely have been the beginning of an elaborate game of make-believe. Just a month, but so much had changed. Their pretend games of wizards and magic were now real and wonderful and amazing and, sometimes, frightening. How could they possibly make him understand?

"I don't know Dad," said Nyree, "I just like it 'cos it's a nice place to sit and sketch."

"And it's a fun place to scramble around and explore." Elias pitched in.

"Oh." The smile slipping from Dad's face. "Well, have fun and be careful both of you." He returned to his cup of tea and book.

"Come on Elias," said Nyree softly. "Let's go."

When they reached the tower, the children were astounded by the sight that greeted them. Gone was the half-finished building site they had left. Instead, there was a gleaming tower worthy of any story-book sorcerer. Rough window-holes in the stonework now sparkled with beautifully polished wooden frames. The panes had an other-worldly iridescence.

Yelling their joy to the skies, Elias and Nyree ran through the gate to the tower door where they threw themselves into a hug with a rather startled Malachite.

"It's wonderful!" cried Nyree.

"Amazing!" said Elias.

Malachite smiled, holding them gently. "Well, I am

110

rather pleased with the result, I must say. I hope you don't mind. I made a few amendments to the plans you made. Nothing quite as exciting, but I do hope it will serve. Welcome to the Tower of Sorcery." Malachite straightened and threw open the carved double doors.

They stepped inside and looked around in amazement. The main entrance hall was a single gigantic room occupying the full ground floor of the tower. Stone pillars, carved of a strange semi-translucent rock, created something of a walkway around the edge. The tops were carved to look as if a certain imp was holding up the ceiling. On closer inspection, each carving was in a slightly different pose, some with rather comical facial expressions.

"Brilliant," cackled Elias as he turned to see them all.

In the centre of the room stood the main tower staircase. A double helix of treads twisting around each other spiralling up to the floor above. Looking out from the staircase Nyree could see that the slight rainbow sheen to the windows, which had appeared clear and colourless from every other viewpoint, looked like a series of stained glass windows each showing different scenes of Nyree building the tower with magic.

Elias stepped into the centre of the stair-well and leaped to the next floor.

"Come on Nyree, let's explore!" he called back.

"Show off," muttered Nyree, stepping into the open space. With a quick burst of magic, she floated up to join her brother.

On the next floor, the landing opened onto a comfortable lounge area. Almost half the remaining floor space was given over to a ballroom area. The other side of the lounge was taken up by an enormous dining hall. Opposite the lounge, occupying almost a quarter arc of the tower, was what looked like a kitchen.

"It occurred to me," said Malachite as he cleared the final steps to join them, "that we hadn't given much consideration to entertaining guests in our initial designs."

"It's wonderful, Malachite," said Nyree, "but when will we possibly use all this? There must be space for hundreds of people here."

"Nyree, don't burst Mal's bubble," scolded Elias. "If he wants to dream of having faery hoards over for a bit of lunch, you should let him."

"Well, children," smiled Malachite, "time will tell."

"Onward and upward?" asked Elias.

Nyree held Malachite in her gaze for a moment. She wondered what secret future he knew or guessed at. When no answers appeared, she drifted up to the next floor.

"Onward and upward, young master." Malachite began his rather slower climb up the stairs. With an excited whoop, Elias leaped up the stair well after Nyree.

A library filled the next level. Although, using the same word for this place and the Duloch public library seemed unreasonable.

Elias gave a whistle. "There must be... wow. How many books do you think there are here?"

Nyree glanced around making a quick count of the

112

bookcases, which split the room like rays on a child's drawing of the sun. She wandered over and picked up some books at random, glancing at the spine size. She cocked her head to the side for a moment, thinking.

"About two hundred and ninety thousand. I think."

"Quite a few then," said Elias.

Nyree drifted dreamlike past the shelves, entirely awestruck by what she saw. She felt her lips move, heard herself say, "Malachite, how did you get all these?"

"You forget, my dear," said Malachite proudly, "that I've been waiting for a rather long time. Much of it has been spent collecting books to help guide you. Many of them seek to explain the magical secrets from various cultures from around the world and throughout history. I have also attempted to gather as much material as possible on the prophesy. My hope was to shed some light on who our enemy might be."

"What did you learn?" asked Nyree.

"Much, and yet very little," sighed Malachite. "There are a few legends about soul-stealers, soul-eaters and the like. The Hausa people of Nigeria tell of soul-eaters. The Striga, of Albanian and ancient Roman legend, were said to feed on a person's life-force. Japan had the Wanyudo, said to steal the souls of unwary travellers. All of them were either defeated long ago, or simply did not exist in the first place."

"So, we're still at square-one on that then?" Nyree slumped a little.

"Well, not entirely," answered Malachite. "I extended my search to include things which could be loosely interpreted as soul-theft. Remember the original prophecy was in a language now long dead. It would be foolish to hold firm to a single translation."

"And?" Nyree looked up, hope returning to her face.

"Again, nothing certain." Malachite smiled gently. "I spent decades researching vampires, succubae and other creatures that steal any manner of life-essence."

"Vampires?" Elias spun around from where he'd been trying to get a glimpse of the next level up. "That would be cool."

"Dead-end, I'm afraid." Malachite rolled his eyes as he saw a grin spread on Elias's face. "No pun intended."

"Why not vampires?" asked Nyree.

"Well, for starters," said Malachite, "most of the vampires are members of the faery courts. Any rogues would have been dealt with long ago."

"But they could be in hiding." Elias's face was alight with excitement. "A secret cult of evil vampires."

"True, that is possible." Malachite regarded Elias thoughtfully. "I will admit that I hadn't considered that."

"What else did you find?" Nyree's hands drifted to the books on the nearest shelf.

"It occurred to me that the prophecy, however translated, put a considerable amount of weight on the idea of knowledge. My latest theories have surrounded beings whose interest is in stealing, controlling or otherwise disrupting thoughts, knowledge and minds."

"Many of them?"

"That depends on how you look at it." Malachite went on, "There have been countless sorcerers who have developed telepathic powers. All of them were entirely mortal, however, and are quite dead. There was also the Cult of Babel, who tried to collect and control all human knowledge. Records of them vanished in biblical times, but I believe some remnants may be awaiting a chance to return. That is, after all, the nature of cults. I also found a few intriguing references to a group called the Coranaid."

"Never heard of them," said Nyree.

"Indeed," Malachite nodded. "There is little material on them. What I have found is confused and contradictory in places. The basic theme is that they can hear everything which is said aloud."

"So, their special power is not being deaf?" Elias sniggered.

"No, you misunderstand." Malachite smiled patiently. "The special power of the Coranaid is that they hear everything which is said aloud, everywhere in the world."

"What's so scary about that?" asked Elias.

"Pretty hard to plot against them." Nyree shivered. "Hard to organise an uprising if you can't speak about it. In fact if it's them – they're listening to this right now."

"Well, we don't know that it is them," said Malachite. "The few sources were muddled at best. Most likely just folklore. They almost certainly have no basis in fact. But…"

"But?" asked Nyree and Elias together.

"But, if the stories are true," mused Malachite, "and they know all that is spoken, planting confusing myths and suppressing others would not be hard for them. It could be that the rarity of information is evidence in itself."

Malachite shook himself, as if trying to fully awaken. "Just the paranoid ramblings of an old fossil, no doubt."

Nyree shivered again. Somehow Malachite's protest of paranoia wasn't entirely convincing. "So where does that leave us, Malachite?"

"Armed with ideas if nothing else. It is my plan to train you as widely as I can to counter whichever threat turns out to be real."

The three of them stood quietly for a moment, pondering Malachite's words. The silence was finally broken by Elias.

"What I want to know is, where were you hiding all these books?" He grinned cheekily. "They weren't all here last time I looked."

"Indeed, not." Malachite turned to Elias. "Many I had in storage, the rest, I distributed among my friends for safe keeping."

"Friends?" said Nyree and Elias together.

"Quite so," said Malachite returning to the stairs, "come along now, we have lots still to see."

⊶⬦⊷

The floor above was split into several apartments. Malachite made a particular point of showing them which one was his private suite. Moving around, Malachite pointed out the apartments he had set aside for Nyree and Elias.

"In case you need quiet time," he said, "while you're training here."

116

Separating the two was a corridor with three doors in it. Those on the sides were access into each of their apartments. At the end of the corridor was a rather grander door set in an archway.

"Hang on a minute," said Nyree, "is that…"

Not waiting for her to finish, Elias bounded off down the passageway and straight through the, luckily unlocked, door. Inside he found the 'Rainbow Turret', the result of Nyree's experiment with colour magic. The entire turret room had been decorated as a comfortable lounge. The boisterous colour scheme of the walls matched with tastefully contrasting shades in the furniture. Hanging on the walls were wild modern-art paintings. Malachite had hung these, unframed and cleverly positioned, to blend in with the caper of colours on the walls themselves.

"Cool action-paintings, Mal," said Elias.

The remainder of the main floor was rounded out with several empty suites of rooms. Each was differently decorated. Pleasantly, though unexcitingly.

"Who are these for Mal?" asked Elias.

"No one in particular," responded Malachite. "It is my hope that we will find allies in the future. It may be that we need to provide lodgings for some of them. At least for a while. It is possible that the wisdom spoken of in the prophecy might be found through friends. There are many wise and powerful beings in the world. With luck, some of them may choose to help us."

Up the next flight of stairs was a variety of spell labs, workshops and practice rooms for every branch and aspect of magic and indeed several rooms for seemingly unrelated crafts: woodwork, textiles, and the like. Making a mental note to come back and explore this level more fully, Nyree joined Elias at the stairs, keen to continue the tour and see the rest of the tower. The secrets could be teased out later.

They were both about to hop quickly up to the next level to continue the exploration when Malachite stopped them.

"Nyree, Elias, wait one moment, please." Malachite looked a little nervous. "There's one more thing I'd like to show you here."

He indicated a discreet door between two workshops.

"I hope you don't mind," said Malachite, not making eye contact with either of them, "but I decided to finish the task you started to the best of my abilities."

He led them through the doorway and down a short passage. It ended with an archway opening onto an unfenced balcony platform. As they approached the balcony it became clear why Malachite had hesitated. Spiralling to the left from the balcony was a short flight of floating stairs leading to a turret hanging apparently unsupported in mid-air.

"Malachite, it's magnificent!" breathed Nyree. "I'm a little nervous, though. How did you do it?"

Malachite chuckled quietly. "Well, I have to say: I cheated."

"Cheated? How?" Nyree stepped over for a closer look.

"Well, it's not really floating at all," Malachite confessed, "in fact, the whole thing is sitting on the sturdiest corbels that magic can provide."

"But they... how?" Nyree crouched, peering into the gap between two steps.

"They're glamoured to be invisible!" crowed Elias, delighted to figure it out before his sister for a change.

"Exactly so, Elias!" Pride glowed on Malachite's face. "I did think about trying to build it with your technique Nyree. I genuinely thought you might have solved the problem, but alas not. In all my many years, I have never even heard of a sorcerer who has been able to catch the wind. I do hope you don't mind the counterfeit. Yours was such a bold attempt that I thought it should be captured in some way."

Nyree smiled. "I feel kind of stupid. Why'd I have to try it the hardest way possible?"

"Don't be so harsh with yourself," rumbled Malachite. "Thinking of simple solutions requires experience and a deep understanding of your own limitations. In time, you will gain the experience. However, to discover new things, sometimes one needs to take the harder path. True greatness is only gained by those who know they will probably fail and make the attempt regardless."

Whereas the previous floors had been completely deserted, the next level was a flurry of activity. Dozens of

119

little people, about the size of three-year-olds, bustled around carrying out all manner of domestic task. Although as small as children their wrinkled faces and skin, hairy almost to the point of fur, told another tale.

"Nyree, Elias, meet the brownies." Malachite turned to the one who seemed to be in charge. "Feally, come meet the masters of the tower."

"Sorry, Malachite," said Nyree, "I didn't quite catch that. Felly, did you say?"

"Close enough, mistress" said the head brownie, "although the Sassenachs would have it 'Feldy', never could figure out why."

"As in 'Aberfeldy'," asked Elias, wishing he had something better to add.

"Very good young master," said Feally, "that town is indeed named originally as 'the place of Pheallaidh', being the name of the ancient king of the brownie folk, of whom I am absolutely no relation." Feally swept into an elaborate bow.

"What's with all this 'master' stuff anyway?" asked Elias.

"Well," said Feally, standing back up, "legend has it that one would be chosen to be the saviour of magic and master of the last tower of sorcery. It's my guess that that last tower of sorcery would be this one, I've certainly heard of no other. That would make you the masters here. I guess the legends lost count."

"We can't be having any of that bowing nonsense," said Nyree. "By the looks of it, this is your home. You shouldn't bow to anyone here. And don't call us 'Master'."

"And you canna go messing with nature, mistress," replied Feally without missing a beat. "It is in our nature to serve in domestic chores, so serve we shall. Besides, it is our honour to serve here of all places."

"Well, I guess you can serve." A frown creased Nyree's brow. She didn't like the idea that someone was beneath her. "That doesn't mean you're a servant, though. If housework makes you happy that's fine, but only as a helpful friend. Okay?"

"Where'd you get this one, Malachite?" Feally stage-whispered, not so softly, "she'd change the world given half a chance."

"That, my friend," rumbled Malachite, "was the idea."

Chapter 12

Guests

They covered the rest of the tower in a brisk blur, glimpsing but not exploring. A faery gymnasium for Elias to practice his impish clambering and leaping skills. Empty space reserved for future needs. The roof held an observation deck, equipped with an array of astronomical instruments ranging from sextants and astrolabes to several sophisticated looking telescopes.

Nyree stroked the telescope gently, daydreaming about late star-gazing sessions. Elias leaned out, studying the tower wall for climbing routes. A twinkling light caught their attention. It flitted erratically from the treeline and across the courtyard. It climbed the tower, spiralling back and forth and pausing momentarily, as if checking in the windows.

"We're up here Faltha," yelled Elias.

The light changed direction abruptly and headed

directly for the top. Faltha landed on the parapet next to Nyree.

"Welcome back kids," said Faltha. "Pretty impressive place you have here, isn't it?"

"We've just finished the tour." Elias wrenched his gaze back from the wall and over to Faltha. "Liking it so far."

"You know," Faltha's wheedling tone suggested that this wasn't a new idea she was having, "there's a good view from up here. I bet with a tower like this, I could monitor the wishes in this area much more effectively."

"Faltha," sighed Nyree, "If you want some space here, why not just say so?"

"You really mean it?" asked Faltha, keeping up the pretence.

"Oh, for goodness' sake," said Nyree. "Of course! Although, it's not my home. Malachite?"

"I am sure that some small space can be found." Malachite didn't sound pleased.

"Malachite," said Nyree gently. "We are looking to gather allies. Shouldn't we start by helping the ones we already have?"

"We are," sighed Malachite. "You are, of course, quite right. I struggle with her flighty flippancy, though."

"You know, I'm standing right here," grumbled Faltha.

"This is a serious place, with a serious purpose," continued Malachite, "not a faery playground. It starts with one faery..."

"Who has a name!" Faltha's wings fluttered angrily.

"...and before you know it, there's a minor troupe in residence."

"It won't be like last time," snapped Faltha.

"Last time?" asked Nyree.

"Several years ago," replied Malachite, "Faltha and a group of other faeries came to work here. For a time, I was glad of the company..."

"You didn't look it," interrupted Faltha.

"I was concentrating. I thought I might have stumbled on an important lead. Faltha and her friends took it upon themselves to 'cheer me up.'"

"What happened?" asked Nyree.

"Well, things got a little out of hand." Unexpectedly, Faltha blushed and lowered her wings. "We might have slightly set fire to his rose garden."

"And knocked down a wall and collapsed my bed-chamber," rumbled Malachite.

"I said I was sorry," mumbled Faltha.

"I was sleeping in it at the time."

"I'm sorry Malachite," said Nyree. "I shouldn't have suggested giving her a room here."

"It's okay, Nyree," said Malachite. "You were correct. We need allies in this. It is proper that we help them where we can."

"Okay then." Nyree's shoulders relaxed slightly. "Faltha, set up in the floating turret for now. That place still freaks me out a little. But Faltha," Nyree added as she spotted the beginning of Faltha's triumphant smile. "Play nice."

"Umm, guys?" Elias was looking over the parapet

125

again. "You might want to see this."

Everyone looked where Elias was pointing at the treeline. A spider scuttled out from the undergrowth. A spider they could see from nine floors up. *It's like something out of a fairy-tale*, Nyree mused with a sideways glance at Faltha and Malachite. A wry smile creased her lips.

"Ah, now there's a face I haven't seen in a long time..." Malachite turned and leaped into the gap in the centre of the stairwell, dropping the entire height of the tower.

"That looks fun!" Elias grinned after his teacher for a moment.

"Elias, don't you dare!" shouted Nyree.

"I was just saying..." Elias turned away from the stairs. He smirked then climbed over the wall and followed the route that he had, mostly, planned down the outer face of the tower.

∽∻❀∻∾

To say that the spider was huge didn't really do the creature justice. Standing a metre tall, its spindly legs were as thick as drainpipes. The arrangement of its eight eyes suggested it was a jumping spider, in the same way that a velociraptor was a prehistoric turkey.

"Cauldron, my old friend!" Malachite boomed as he crossed the courtyard. He spread his arms wide, as if to hug the beast.

"Malachite!" To Nyree's surprise the spider could

126

speak. Its voice was ancient and rasping, yet somehow lively. Full of vigour and joy. "I see you've been busy, old boy!" it added, apparently taking in the newly rebuilt tower.

"Indeed," replied Malachite closing the final distance. He aimed a bear-crushing embrace at his friend, which Cauldron deftly dodged while cleverly managing to look like he was bowing in greeting. "In truth, most of the work was carried out by my young friends here," Malachite gestured at the children, "Cauldron, meet Nyree and Elias, the new masters of the tower."

"Well, well," said Cauldron, looking them over carefully. "So, you two are who all the fuss is about then?"

"Fuss, sir?" asked Nyree. She hoped that polite ignorance was the best approach to take when talking with a giant spider.

"Well yes. The whole magical world has been turned on its head. Rumours, evidently true, of the return of a Tower of Magic. Reports of increased tensions between the faery courts." Catching the look on Malachite's face, Cauldron added, "Worse than usual, I mean. The Great Library in Tibet was burned to the ground by forces unknown. There has been talk from all over of trolls wandering down from the mountains and causing havoc. I hear rumour that the goblin war-bands are reforming. Now it seems that your end of the prophecy is unfolding. A new sorcerer, and if I am not mistaken a new faery prince, have arrived on the scene. I believe the time has come to take sides, my friend, and so here I am."

"Those are grim tidings indeed, Cauldron," said

Malachite. "The Library is a terrible loss. I can confirm the rumours of trolls are true. We have encountered some. On the very day that Nyree and Elias were chosen, no less. I fear you may be right. The enemy may at last be moving against us and our own preparations are still very much in their infancy."

"Don't despair, my friend. I believe there is still time. Once the enemy's plans are in motion, I expect there will be no doubting it." Cauldron paused for a moment, shuffling to inspect Nyree and Elias once more, "For what it's worth, I will help as I may. You're not alone in this fight."

"We would be delighted for your help, sir," Nyree said. She couldn't settle on which of Cauldron's many eyes to look at. Eventually she picked one of the largest pair. "I hope you don't mind, but… what help are you offering?"

"Of course, of course," responded Cauldron as if only just realising that it wasn't entirely obvious. "I have some skills in the brewing of magical potions. A fascinating craft, in my opinion. At the height of sorcery, it had fallen almost entirely out of fashion. However, remains a worthy art. I would very much like the opportunity to teach it to you."

"That sounds amazing," said Nyree. "Please, come on in. I'm sure Malachite and the brownies can find you suitable rooms to stay in. Do you have much luggage with you?"

"No, my dear," said Cauldron, "nothing but the clothes on my back and the wit and wisdom in my mind!"

Nyree gave an uncomfortable chuckle. Being a spider, Cauldron wasn't wearing any clothes but was instead covered in loose, hairy fur ranging from a deep midnight black to russet brown.

"Supplies for potion making then?" hazarded Nyree. Nothing in her life so far had prepared her to welcome a giant, talking spider. She hoped she was doing it right.

"Nothing with me, sadly," sighed Cauldron. "Long distance travel is such a bother; carrying a collection of bottles would be most prohibitive."

"Travel indeed," said Malachite. "Last I'd heard, you were touring around Mexico terrifying the native wise-men into giving up their tribal secrets."

"Brazil actually," replied Cauldron. "I'd moved on to harassing the Amazon tribes. You would not believe the magic those people were hiding. Amazing."

Chapter 13

Potions

Nyree and Elias were at the tower early the next morning. The appearance of Cauldron, and all the possibilities he brought, had relit their enthusiasm for all things magical. Besides which, Nyree had reasoned, learning potions was bound to be safer than magical architecture.

"Good morning, children," called Malachite when they entered the tower. "Cauldron and I have been discussing your ongoing education. We have decided that it would be best to get you a grounding in potions as quickly as possible."

"So, for the next few days," continued Cauldron, "you both will study exclusively with me. After that, we can relax into a more balanced division of your time and allow you to work more according to your tastes and needs. Malachite has set me up with an excellent potion laboratory on the fifth floor, and the brownies have provided all the supplies we will need, at least to get started. When you are ready, please join me there."

Cauldron leaped up the stair well. He flicked out a line of silk and pulled himself up out of sight.

"It's just like we're back at school again," groaned Elias.

"I know, great isn't it!" Excitement built in Nyree's voice. "Although when did you ever fly at school?"

In the fifth-floor lab, three large wooden workbenches had been arranged to form an open triangle near the centre of the room. On each was a stout cauldron suspended on a tripod, as well as a variety of glassware, stirring instruments and racks for bottles and such. The centre of the room contained an enormous cauldron suspended by a chain from the ceiling.

"Wow! Look at that thing." Elias circled around the cauldron. "We could probably both fit in there."

"I wouldn't recommend it." Cauldron's voice floated down from the shadows above. "We'll be brewing some extremely potent mixtures in there. It would be best to avoid any accidents."

Cauldron drifted down a strand of web to land deftly on his workbench. "Welcome to the potions lab. In here I shall teach you what I believe is the greatest of the sorcerous arts."

"Sorry to interrupt, Cauldron," said Nyree, "but how come Malachite hasn't mentioned it before?"

"No need to apologise at all my dear," replied Cauldron. His voice might have suggested a smile, if only he had a human mouth. "Indeed, although it is regarded by some as the greatest art, it is often overlooked by sorcerers. You see, ultimately the art of potions is to locate and unleash the trapped inner magic of mundane objects. Because of this there are relatively few effects which can be produced by potions that cannot be achieved by 'regular' sorcery. Thus, many shun the art as essentially a side-show. Even if potions offered a greater range than sorcery, many have found that the intricate interaction of ingredients to be tiresome compared to the freedom of effect following thought. To some, the delivery mechanism is also somewhat wanting. After all, one must either drink a potion, or be splashed with it to release the magic."

"Okay," said Nyree, "those are some compelling reasons why we wouldn't want to learn potions. Where's the however?"

"However," Cauldron's voice was like a mischievous grin, "these are also great advantages. You see, replacing imagination with a systematic interaction of substances makes it susceptible to analysis. No longer is the magic constrained by the intellect of the wielder. Similarly, a potion takes no concentration to use. One can work the magic years, even centuries, in advance of using it. Additionally, the potion's potency is not limited by the power of the user. Indeed, consider how you are both here today."

"Malachite splashed us both with a potion." Elias's eyes grew wide as he thought this through.

"Quite so," replied Cauldron. "And although I respect Malachite greatly as a sorcerer, and love him like a brother, I contend that he doesn't have the power to turn one, even naturally gifted, girl into a wizard let alone fully transform a boy into one of the faery folk."

"How far does this go?" asked Elias.

"I'm sorry, what do you mean?" replied Cauldron, although it sounded like he knew exactly what Elias was thinking.

"You said that it isn't limited by the magical strength of the user. How far does that go?"

Cauldron made a slight bobbing motion, which might have been the spider equivalent of a nod. "Would you like to find out?"

His back leg scooped up a bottle from the table with a luminescent blue liquid inside and he dexterously flipped it over to Elias, who caught the bottle and paused for a moment.

"But I can't use sorcery at all," he mumbled before popping the lid off and taking a gulp.

"Which is hardly less than I—" said Cauldron, before interrupting himself, "Ah, sorry, I meant to say: just a small sip will do."

As the potion passed his lips, Elias felt a strange buzzing sensation. Otherwise, everything seemed normal.

"Now go for a walk around the room." Cauldron spoke in the slow deliberate voice that grown-ups sometimes use for particularly difficult children.

With a huff of annoyance, Elias started to walk. As he set off, he noticed that Nyree seemed to be feigning astonishment. Her jaw dropped with mocking slowness. Then he noticed the potion bottle. He'd casually dropped it on the table as he started to walk, and yet it was still hanging in the air where he'd let go of it. *Interesting* he thought, then set off at a run. As he neared the first wall, an idea occurred to him. He ran straight up the wall, over the ceiling, and down the other wall. He dodged past Nyree and came back to his desk in plenty of time to catch the dropped bottle before it had travelled the short distance to the desk. A few seconds later, the buzzing sensation faded and everyone else seemed to catch up.

"Nice one!" Elias grinned. "I think I'm going to like potions really quite a lot."

Cauldron spent the remainder of the morning teaching Nyree and Elias about how various ingredients embody different characteristics that are then blended to produce the desired effect from the potion.

"For example," said Cauldron, "our speed potion from earlier used the primary feather of a peregrine falcon and a cheetah hair for speed. To this I added a hummingbird feather for control and stability. That part was particularly important for indoor use. There was also a final ingredient, which I must admit is a recent innovation of my own, some spider silk for traction. With the original formulation, the drinker could go exceedingly fast, but turning proved to be quite an issue."

"Let me guess," said Elias, "the base liquid was

quick-silver?"

"Dear goodness, no!" cried Cauldron. "Mercury is extremely poisonous. You must never use such things in potions. No, while we are unlocking the underlying magic of the ingredients we use, their mundane properties still stand."

"In other words," said Nyree, "if you've got a nut allergy, don't get an impact resistant shell by using peanuts."

"Quite so my dear, quite so."

"So, what did you use?" asked Elias.

"Well, in this case, just water." Seeing that this was an unsatisfyingly simple answer, Cauldron continued, "You see, water as a base liquid is most helpful, especially for novices to the craft. In terms of its magical potential water is relatively inert, so using it has little effect on the magic of the potion."

"Okay, cool." said Elias thoughtfully.

"I think now might be as good a time as any to break for lunch," said Cauldron. "Shall we meet back here in an hour?"

Chapter 14

Blood and Power

Cauldron and Nyree left the lab deep in conversation about why peregrine and cheetah samples in potions, when clearly there are far faster objects in the world.

"Essentially," said Cauldron, "it's a question of personal taste. Well, that and keeping the demonstration under control. I couldn't very well have Elias going so fast that he'd crash straight through the wall of my nice new lab, now could I?"

As they stepped out of the room an idea occurred to Elias. *A slowing potion could be fun to have,* he thought, *especially as a revenge prank on Malachite for his slow spell 'accident'.*

He slipped over to the ingredients shelves by the wall and started to have a rummage through. After about five minutes of browsing, he returned to his workbench, arms laden with sloth claw, treacle, tortoise shell, sloe junipers, which sounded right at least, and his personal favourite: a drop of tar. He dropped a sample of each into his cauldron and measured out a suitable quantity of what Cauldron had called 'Intense Thermodynamic Concentration potion' into the dish underneath.

It was wonderful stuff. Cauldron had originally designed it for mountain rescue teams to warm up avalanche victims. Then he'd realised that it could be distilled, which massively increased the heat delivered. So much cleaner and more effective than oil lamps and fires for cooking potions in the lab.

The Heat-Mix, as Elias had taken to calling it, much to Cauldron's dismay, did its job quickly and soon Elias's potion was bubbling nicely. He ladled some into a bottle and popped a stopper in then started for the door.

Just as he grabbed the handle it occurred to Elias that he should probably test the potion before pouring it on Malachite. It would be embarrassing if it didn't work. Come to think of it, the potion could do something quite horrible by mistake. It should definitely be tested first.

He carefully dripped a little onto a marble that he happened to have in his pocket, then used a spatula to nudge it across the desk. No effect. Nothing. The marble rolled smoothly across the workbench and clattered to the floor.

In a frustrated rage, Elias threw the bottle down on his worktop. He knew he shouldn't and felt a flash of guilt, but sometimes you just need to break something.

The bottle smashed on the desk. A bouncing shard of glass nicked Elias's hand fractions of a second before the potion splashed him. As Elias tried to snatch his hand away there was a blinding flash. He tried to jump back away from whatever was happening, but he couldn't move.

The thing that annoyed Elias, this time around, was that what he wanted to do most was pick something up, preferably something breakable, and hurl it at the wall screaming curses of frustration. Of course, moving fast enough to do any of that was essentially impossible. Again.

On the upside, the potion seemed to be a complete success. It occurred to Elias to wonder why it only worked after he smashed the bottle. On reflection, if just mixing up that kind of stuff and cooking it was enough on its own, surely it would have been discovered by non-magical people by now. Cauldron had said that after lunch they would learn how to activate the potions. Elias wondered if his imp-blood could do that.

Elias spent the next forty minutes giving potion-craft some careful consideration. As soon as the potion wore off, he swigged a mouthful of Cauldron's speed potion and set to clearing up the mess. That done, another mouthful sent him fleeing downstairs to grab a quick bite to eat from the kitchen. The brownies looked quite startled when a large plate of sandwiches leaped off the counter and out the door in a blur of blue.

Nyree and Cauldron came back into the potions lab to find Elias sitting at his bench idly thumbing through a rather hefty book of ingredients and their properties.

"Oh," said Nyree, "you got back fast. Or have you not left at all yet? We missed you at lunch. What have you been up to?"

"Nothing." said Elias, smiling sweetly and mustering

probably the least innocent expression ever worn by anyone.

⚬⚬✦⚬⚬

Once they had settled back in, Cauldron set out a pair of books. 'An Introduction to Potions' was carved onto the leather bindings.

"Huh," Nyree stroked the book lovingly, "just like a real wizards' school."

"Indeed," said Cauldron nodding. Nyree was nearly certain that was a nod this time. "I rescued these from a schoolhouse used by a witches' coven long ago, when it closed rather suddenly. I gave them to Malachite for safe keeping. Dark times, such dark times," he wobbled sadly as he said the last part, as a human might shake his head. "Anyway, I think it is high time you mix your own potions. Then I will show you how to activate them. Turn to page twelve and assemble the ingredients you find there."

Nyree and Elias opened their books and started gathering the ingredients for the unimaginatively named 'light potion' found on page twelve. Nyree balanced the open book on her arm and started meticulously scouring the shelves for the ingredients listed. Meanwhile, Elias gave the page a quick glance, nodded once and sprang off, grabbing bottles as he skipped briskly around the shelves.

"Elias! Will you watch out," shouted Nyree after the third time he jostled past her.

"Sorry. Just excited." Elias reached around her to grab another bottle. "This potion stuff is really cool."

By the time Nyree had collected all the supplies she needed, Elias's potion was already quietly bubbling. Nyree hurriedly mixed the ingredients together and, so not to be totally bested by her brother, ignored Cauldron's heat-mix and instead sent a small burst of magic to warm her pot to a rolling boil.

"Well done both of you," said Cauldron after giving each mixture a sniff. "Both seem well prepared and sufficient to be getting on with. Now, to activate a potion one needs simply to provide it with magical power. When you have put in enough magic there will be a small flash of light, at that point stop and the potion will be ready."

"Oh," Nyree bit her lip and gave her brother a sidelong glance. "That means you can't finish it Elias. I guess I'll have to help you with this bit."

"Well do your one first." Elias's face was a masterpiece of unconcern. "Once you've got that right, we can see about you helping me."

Nyree turned and reached her hand toward her potion, readying her magic. Elias pulled a small leather packet from his pocket and fished out a long sewing pin. A small jab at his index finger drew the desired drop of blood. A quick squeeze of his finger and it dripped into his cauldron with a barely audible plink.

Cauldron whipped around, spider-fast. "What was that?" he started to say when the whole lab was flooded with a searing white light. He shot across the lab and leaned alarmingly close to Elias's face. "What did you do? Tell me!" he shouted as the light began to fade.

"Um, just dripped a little blood into it." said Elias,

flinching away from Cauldron's nightmarish face.

"You… hmm. Interesting." Cauldron moved back and sank his body to the desk, presumably the spider equivalent of sitting. "I've never actually heard of faeries practising potion craft before. Naturally, your blood would activate a potion. It is, for want of a better way of putting it, made of magic. My boy this is completely ground-breaking." He paused for a moment, considering. "You know, don't tell anyone about this. If word got out that faery blood was all that was needed to make magic, well I think that would change the world, and not necessarily for the better."

"Okay," Elias settled back into his seat. "So, you just did a whole thing there by yourself. Give me a moment to catch up."

"Don't you understand, Elias?" A worried look spread over Nyree's face. "If non-magical people found out about this, they would hunt faeries to harvest their blood. They'd be able to make potions – who knows what for. With the sheer number of people, how long do you think the faeries would last? They'd be hunted to extinction in no time."

"Okay," Elias frowned, "so we keep the secret. I can still make potions though, right?"

"Well," said Cauldron, "so long as you only practise within this room. Tell no one, not even the brownies. No one must know but the three of us."

"Wouldn't it make sense for me to just activate Elias's potions?" asked Nyree. "That way, he can be seen to brew potions and let me activate them. It would actually strengthen the secret, I think."

"Yeah. Good idea, sis." A half smile formed on Elias's lips. "Means I don't need to keep jabbing myself, too."

Chapter 15

Gifts

Nyree was fascinated by the scientific potential of potions. Her methodical approach to the subject seemed to delight her teacher. The intense discussions between Nyree and Cauldron frequently resulted in his scurrying away to make some notes or follow up on a line of research.

On her second day in the potion lab, Nyree started an experiment to understand how using different base liquids would alter the properties of potions brewed using precisely the same quantities of identical ingredients. She had even gone as far as making sure that each herb used was cut from a single plant for all the potions, ensuring the same strength each time.

If Nyree's potion brewing skills were impressive, Elias was nothing short of a genius. Although, as with most things, 'systematic' held little interest for Elias, his instinct seemed to unerringly guide him. After two days, Elias was starting to produce potions which Cauldron, with his many years of study, had never heard of. His method seemed to involve bustling around the lab in a blue blur of activity, any pretence at human appearance fallen to the wayside, all the while flinging ingredients into his cauldron with a wild abandon. For all that, luck seemed to have no role in the process. Whenever Cauldron challenged him to produce a particular effect, the desired potion appeared quickly and without flaw.

While most of his potions were, as agreed, powered by Nyree's magic, a few lunch-time experiments were entirely his own work and activated with imp blood. One such experiment resulted in an intriguing paint which would change hue if someone were to touch it and concentrate on a new colour. He had hoped to repaint the so called 'colour-turret', claiming that the horrific mash-up of colours gave him a headache. Malachite, however, forbade any such redecoration, branding it as wanton vandalism.

One morning, as Nyree and Elias strolled up to the tower, laughing and joking as they went, they were approached by Feally and a small group of brownies.

"Master, Mistress." The brownie bowed low before straightening to look them each in the eye. "My friends and I made you these gifts, as thanks for dealing so kindly with us. We hope that they will help on the path ahead of you."

He gestured to one of the others, who stepped forward carrying a long object wrapped loosely in cloth.

The brownie bowed in front of Nyree before kneeling and holding the package out.

Nyree unwrapped the cloth to see a beautifully carved wooden staff. As she lifted it from the brownie's outstretched hands, she felt a familiar hum of magic within the wood.

"Feally!" Nyree gasped, "this was my flying stick! Oh, this is wonderful, I love it. Thank you so much." Nyree propped the staff up in the air and felt a fleeting pride at how effortless magic was becoming. She hugged the brownie who had held it and then grabbed Feally in an embrace so ferocious he yelped in surprise.

"There's a setting at the top for a gem-stone, or some other ornament," said Feally once he'd escaped from Nyree's arms and caught his breath. "We weren't sure of your tastes, so we left it empty for now. If it would please you to help us design something, we'd love to finish the job."

He turned to Elias and gestured over his shoulder. Another brownie stepped out of the group and with the same bowing and kneeling, held out another cloth-bound gift. This one substantially smaller than the other, fitting neatly into the brownie's upheld hands.

"Thanks everyone!" Elias shot them a grin and flipped back the cloth to reveal a small black lump with an orange gem set into it.

"Um, not to sound ungrateful," Elias looked curiously at the object, "but, what is it?"

"Of course, young master," said the gift bearer, "let me explain. We had heard of your talent for potion-brewing and devised a portable cauldron for you. Press the gem to see."

Elias held a breath and reached out his hand to touch the gem. For a moment nothing happened. Then, with the slightest of hisses, the lump unfolded, stretched, and formed into an ornate cauldron the size of a football. Its outer surface had been etched with images of an imp dancing around a cauldron which bubbled with some magic brew.

"Now tap the rim," the brownie said.

Elias duly tapped the rim. From the point where his finger struck the metal, a trace of red spread around then fell in glowing arcs to the base of the cauldron. The orange gemstone, which sat at the bottom of the pot, blazed with light.

"A fire opal," said Feally. "It's an old brownie trick. We can make fire opals give out as much heat as a great flame." He smiled at that then continued, "it's most helpful for warming up wash-water and for pressing clothes nice and flat."

"Feally, it is truly amazing," Elias shook his head in disbelief, "but how did you make it? Brownies are a kind of faery, right? So, you can't use sorcery but there's obviously some magic going on here."

"Ah," Feally nodded wisely, "well, we're quite unusual for faeries. In fact, there are some in the courts that don't consider us proper faeries at all." Elias frowned at this but allowed Feally to continue. "That's daft though. We're an embodiment of magic, same as anyone. And just like everyone and everything, the magic touches us in a way that suits our nature. Sprites and the like have the Glamour. The Wild Hunt have gifts of might and stealth. There are others that can see the future. Our magic suits us well. It creates order around us. Tidies up, if you like. We just applied that rather cleverly to the wee pot there, and, well, you see the result."

"Thank you, so much." Elias's voice shook slightly as he said this.

"Really, there's no need." Feally blushed as he spoke. "Just follow his example. That will be thanks enough."

"Example?"

"The Great Imp," said Feally in a reverent tone. "Brownie lore tells us that he too was a great brewer of potions. We never thought the world would see his like again, and yet…"

"So, no pressure then!" said Elias, before squeezing Feally in an exuberant hug of his own.

Elias bounded up the stairwell with his usual lunatic enthusiasm for movement. His portable cauldron was once more compressed and tucked under his arm. He was excited to show off his new treasure to Faltha. He was also eager to hear what she knew about the Great Imp. She had mentioned him before but, somehow, they got distracted before getting into any detail. It was curious, now he thought about it. The Great Imp was a legend among faeries and supposedly renowned for his potions, yet Cauldron was seemingly unaware of faeries brewing potions.

As he neared the floating turret, Elias slowed down. He had a sudden realisation that perhaps Faltha might not enjoy him charging into what had become her private space in the tower. Elias was guiltily aware that since he'd discovered potions, he had been somewhat neglectful of Faltha, Glamours and all things faery. He decided that he should try to make it up to her, starting with being a little less intrusive.

So, breaking with tradition, Elias quietly walked to the door of the floating turret and paused for a moment, listening in case even knocking would disturb Faltha.

"… just think Grunda." Faltha's voice was raised, excited. "This could be the break I need to get some real influence at court! I mean look at this. A permanent presence in the last tower of sorcery! Getting the chosen ones on our side! One of them's practically my protégé for goodness' sake! I'm on a roll."

Elias took half a step back. *Should I really be listening in on this?* he wondered. *Probably not.* As he turned away another voice started.

"Well played indeed, sister!" Grunda, presumably, giggled. "A wish monitoring station! And they believed that! How wonderful. And that boy! What have you told him to have him wrapped around your finger so?"

"Grunda." Faltha sounded a little indignant. "I have told them not one word of a lie. Wish monitoring is, in fact, still my official court position."

"For now!" put in Grunda.

"Well indeed." Faltha was practically purring. "But

should my position change and my needs alter I'm sure that Nyree and Elias won't put me out."

"Doesn't hurt that the place is a veritable stronghold against the Unseelies when shove turns to strike, though," crowed Grunda. "I can't imagine that the Court would mind convening at 'Faltha's Tower' when trouble swings around again."

Elias was glued to the spot. This sounded like something he needed to hear, whether he should or not.

"I'm pleased about that, I must confess." Faltha's voice was quieter now – Elias could feel his ear growing slightly as his imp powers sharpened his senses. "But it's not as if I'm taking advantage of them." She paused. Her next words were murmured at the edge of hearing. "Not completely."

"The amount of advantage you've taken, for yourself as well as for the whole court, is quite simply staggering, my dear." Grunda's shrill, arrogance was really starting to annoy Elias.

"Gained, Grunda, gained." Faltha was starting to sound agitated. "I've *taken* nothing."

"Ha—" Grunda started, but Faltha cut her off.

"I've trained Elias faithfully, and to the best of my abilities. I have paid for every advantage I've obtained and even if there were none…" She paused, calming down a little, "Och, you should see that boy Grunda. He's a sight to see! I'd follow him to the ends of the earth if it came to it. I swear I'd follow him if it meant turning on the court itself."

Stunned silence followed this. Moments dripped by like the turning of the ages. Finally, Grunda spoke: "Don't even joke about that! It's a good thing he's an asset to the court, or we could both get in serious trouble for you even joking about that."

A brief pause, then Faltha spoke again, strong and clear this time, "I swear by my blood and by my glamour that I will follow him, even if it means being banished from the Seelie Court of Faeries."

It was as if time itself held its breath at the touch of those words.

The stillness was broken by Grunda. "You selfish wee pixie!" she hissed. "Did you even think how an oath like that would affect me? Are you mad? A blood oath? From my own sister, no less! Even hearing a thing like that could destroy my standing at court!"

Elias slipped away, as silent as an absence, his mind churning with what he'd heard.

Chapter 16

Goblins

Nyree was at the other side of the tower with Malachite in the Enchantment room. Over the last week Malachite had cleared one of the general-purpose workshops and set it up as a room dedicated to imbuing objects with magic. The walls were lined with racks and shelves filled with a selection of easy to enchant items: crystals, wands, rings, goblets, belts, gloves, anything which could even be imagined as magical was represented. In the centre of the room stood an ingenious contraption which could be adjusted to support any of those objects and present them as an easy target for sorcery. Surrounding that mediaeval-looking device was a set of positively modern blast shields, wisely obtained by Malachite 'against the sheer inevitability of an experiment failing violently'.

Nyree's new staff was clamped upright in the stand. Nyree and Malachite circled it, admiring the craftsmanship of the brownies from every angle.

"Simply wonderful." Malachite leaned in, gazing at the knot patterns weaving intricately around each other. "You see how there are actually three distinct knot patterns?" he gestured at the wood.

"Oh, cool!" Nyree peered closely at her staff. "I hadn't noticed before but look. The three knot strands actually form a knot pattern themselves!"

They both took a quiet moment, their eyes tracing the carvings along the staff.

"I still haven't figured out what I want on the top yet." Nyree gazed up at the metal bands ringing the top and transitioning smoothly, magically, into the sculpted wood.

"There's no need to rush." Malachite looked thoughtful. "I think in the fullness of time the right design will reveal itself to you."

"Hmm," huffed Nyree, "that's not at all cryptic." She gave Malachite a questioning look, but Malachite had stonewalling down to a fine art.

"Anyway," she continued, "putting extra enchantments into it. That's possible, right?"

"Certainly," said Malachite, shaking himself as if out of a daydream, "broadly speaking, it's the same process as before."

"It's the 'broadly speaking' part that seems to get me in trouble."

"Well, quite." Malachite paused. A thoughtful frown creased his brow. "Adding the additional enchantments themselves is achieved in the same way as with the first. However, the problem is one of accessing the magic once it is embodied in the staff. When there are multiple sorceries applied to an object, simply providing magical energy to that object would, of course, power all the enchantments at once."

"Of course," said Nyree. Mostly without a mocking tone.

"To access enchantments separately, one must attach to each a key." Malachite continued as if Nyree hadn't spoken, "This key is a distinct thought bound to the desired enchantment. To activate a particular enchantment, one simply thinks of the key and provides power."

"Okay, sounds easy enough."

"As is so often the case, something sounding easy doesn't make it so." Malachite cautioned her, "in this case, the trick is thinking the key thought at the same time as sending magic to lock the enchantment in."

"Ah, I see," Nyree grimaced, "the old 'do two things at once' trick. Maybe I should hold off for a bit."

"I'm glad to see that you're learning," Malachite chuckled, "but in this case, there is actually an easy trick to it."

"I guess that had to happen eventually."

"The trick is," Malachite went on, "to say a particular key word as you fix the enchantment. Then to use the staff, you would simply say the word aloud, or with practice in your mind, and provide some power."

"Okay, that actually does sound easy." A flicker of worry danced across Nyree's forehead. "Do I have to remove the flying enchantment first and start again?"

"No, you shouldn't have to." Malachite smiled

gently. "Hold the staff and recall the mental pattern for flying, then say 'fly' and fix the enchantment."

Nyree did so, then gave the staff a brief test. "So far so good!"

"Now add another," said Malachite. "Try illumination. That should be useful."

Nyree pressed in an illumination spell and set the key as 'shine'. Nyree tilted her head, considering what else would be useful. It was, she supposed, like designing a swiss-army knife. After the obvious tools, the question was how to cover every need with as few things as possible. In quick succession she called out, "Heat… Shield… Bump," adding corresponding enchantments for heat, a barrier, and for moving objects around. She leaned back against one of the blast shields and considered what to add next.

"Well done," said Malachite, "you seem to have grasped that fairly well. Now—"

A commotion at the outer gate interrupted whatever Malachite was about to say. He and Nyree raced to the window and burst out onto the balcony together.

"Goblins!" cried Malachite, "Up to no good, by the look of things. I shall see them off."

He leaped from the balcony, landed heavily on the grass, and charged at the intruders.

A horde of wiry greenish creatures were seething in through the gateway. The iron gate lay twisted in ruins on the grass.

Elias burst into the room calling out, "Hey guys, what's going—" he stopped as he saw Nyree grab her staff and fly out the window. "Wait for me!" he shouted, running to follow.

Elias leaped and bounced down the buttresses in staccato hops. He landed on the grass seconds behind Malachite and Nyree.

Malachite crashed straight into the front line of goblins halfway across the courtyard and kept moving, tearing a channel through their midst. The ferocity of his assault seemed to briefly stop the goblins. But as soon as they halted, they started again. Their battle-cry was an ear-cracking shriek. The goblins piled onto Malachite, slowing him by weight of numbers. Even Malachite's tough stone body would surely break under such an attack.

"Nyree," Elias called, running up to her. "I have an idea. Give me some cover!"

Nyree swept her hand across the battlefield. A dense magical fog rolled in completely blocking the combatants from view.

"Hold it a moment," said Elias, eyes closed in concentration. "Okay, lift it. Now."

As Nyree dropped her hand, the fog dissipated leaving behind an astonishing scene of chaos. A small number of goblins had seemingly been replaced by Elias, Malachite and even some brownies in places.

"Your doing?" Nyree asked.

"Yup!" Proud mirth wrinkled Elias's eyes.

Looking at the battle again, Nyree could see that the goblins had turned on each other. Their deadly swords and brutal clubs were now used against friends that suddenly looked like enemies.

"The real art to it," said Elias, "is giving them just enough targets to cause chaos, without making so many that they see through the trick."

"Nice one!" Nyree was grinning too, then glanced from the battle to the outer wall, "uh-oh…"

"What's up?" asked Elias, eyes still fixed on the ground battle.

"I think the guys on the ground were just a decoy."

Elias tore his gaze upward. "You've got to be kidding me! Rocket launchers? What are goblins doing with rocket launchers?"

"Let's ask them." Nyree leaped into the air, pushed power into her staff and flew toward the wall.

Elias bounded in a straight-line path which took him right through the ground fight. At the last moment, skin glistening blue, he hurled himself into the air and in three steps hopped from head to head over the fighters. He made one final leap, intended to take him directly to the top of the wall where the goblins were mustering their long-range troops.

One goblin, somewhat quicker about his business than the rest, managed to fire a shot at Elias. A worryingly large, but surprisingly slow-moving projectile flew lazily at him.

Elias muttered, "I hope this works."

He opened his mouth and swallowed the missile whole. He felt a brief fizzing sensation on his tongue before letting out a smoke-filled burp so forceful that it stopped him in the air. He landed at the base of the outer wall.

Nyree swooped upward just overhead. She hung in the air and yelled, "Bump!"

Sweeping her staff across the ranks of goblins she knocked them all off the wall before landing, a little roughly, next to Elias.

"Nice catch with the rocket!" She shot Elias an excited grin.

"Thanks." Elias grinned back. Adrenaline had kicked in now. He felt awesome and invincible and ready for battle. "But let's deal with this bunch first, yeah?"

They sprang to the top of the wall, just in time to see the next wave of goblins clambering up each other, a writhing green ladder bringing fresh bodies and equipment to the top. Nyree hung back, looking thoughtfully at the oncoming horde. Elias strode forward and grabbed the lead goblin by the wrist. He flung it up into the air and caught it by the ankle. Whipping around Elias used the captive goblin as a club to beat the others back from the wall top.

"Elias!" Nyree yelled, "Try not to hurt them. We don't know why they're attacking. They might have no choice."

"Yeah," Elias shot back, not pausing in his efforts to keep the horde at bay, "but they *are* attacking, and I'd really rather they didn't." He threw his captive/weapon aside and picked up a discarded war-hammer. He grinned as memories of Norse mythology blended with the thrill of the fight.

"Fair point." Nyree glanced at the seething mass of creatures below her. "There has to be a better way though."

"While you're thinking, could you give me a hand?" Elias was slowly losing ground as the intruders managed to gain a foothold on the wall.

"Got it!" Nyree closed her eyes and spread her hands toward the forest. Her brow furrowed in concentration, Nyree send a tidal wave of power over the forest behind the goblins. There was a cracking, swishing sound as a tangle of tentacle vines and leafy branches burst from the treeline grabbing the goblins as it advanced. The animated plant life snatched arms and trapped legs, engulfing, immobilising.

With support from below failing, the living ladder of goblins collapsed under its own weight. The forest continued to roll over the invaders until they were all trapped in a tangled mass.

Nyree sighed and opened her eyes. Her shoulders dropped, and she whispered, "Did I get them all?"

"Nyree." Elias let out a breath which he hadn't realised he was holding. "That was awesome!" He brandished the war-hammer victoriously.

"Now, let's put a stop to the rest of this nonsense, shall we?" Nyree turned to the fight in the courtyard.

"Watch out!" Elias yelled and shoved Nyree off the wall.

Startled fright made Nyree pour magic into her staff. She shot into the air and spun to see what had prompted her brother. A goblin, free from the tangle of its comrades, held a smoking, empty rocket-launcher.

The wall exploded. Tonnes of rock and a little blue imp were thrown into the air. They hung for a moment before falling. So much rock above the limp rag-doll form of her brother.

Nyree launched herself at him like a meteor. Her eyes streamed as the wind raked her face. One clear image filled her vision. A speck of blue against a universe of blurred grey rock. She slammed into Elias with an impact that stole her breath. Desperately hoping that he'd be alright, she yelled, "Shield!" as they bored deep into the collapsing wall.

Malachite was losing. It was a matter of time. There were just so many. He may have been named after a crumbling green gemstone, but Malachite was formed of resolute basalt. He was mighty, but not invincible.

Magic was useless to him in battle. Concentration, born of centuries of discipline, was second nature, but Malachite lacked time. The window of opportunity always snapped shut before he had selected the best spell to apply. So, he fought with fists, feet, and grim disappointment.

His massive fists could crush a goblin like a paper cup, but with a dozen clinging to his arm he could barely move it, let alone swing a punch.

The more he slowed, the more the goblins grappled him. Pounding with their war-hammers. Grinding him down, crying "submit, submit, submit," in their cruel voices. Even as he felt the stone of his arms and chest cracking, he fought on, trapping his attackers in crushing bear-hugs when he could no longer move.

Despite their crippling injuries and the punishing body count, goblins kept coming. When they finally brought Malachite to his knees, the rest of the horde rushed in, heedless of stepping on each other in their frenzy to completely swamp him. Their piercing battle-cry was suddenly drowned out by an explosion.

Desperate strength blossomed in Malachite and he erupted from under the ruck of goblins. Incandescent with rage and terror and hope, he scattered his foes like popping corn. Surely, he hadn't failed. Not after so long waiting.

He looked up in time to see Elias flung high in the air by the blast, surrounded by a torrent of rocks from the ruined wall. A bright streak of light smashed into Elias and buried him deep in the wrecked masonry.

Malachite groaned, sinking to his knees as the goblins renewed their assault. The light seemed to fade from his eyes as he crashed to the ground, crushed at last by despair and the surging bodies of his enemies.

Chapter 17

Preparations

"Elias?" Nyree whispered. "Elias are you okay?"

"Maybe." Came the coughed reply. "Maybe not."

She chuckled at that. "Is there some element of doubt?"

"Well, I had a really weird dream that I was trapped under a collapsing wall." It sounded like Elias sat up.

"Yeah, about that."

"Could you switch the light on, please?" Elias clearly hadn't quite caught up yet. "How come you're in my room so early anyway?"

"Well, you know that dream?" asked Nyree. "It's not really a dream, as such."

"Oh," said Elias, trying not to panic. "Okay, well... light would still be nice. Don't you have a spell for that?"

"Conjuration, as it happens," said Nyree, "and yes, but I'm a little busy running the shield that is keeping all this rock off us."

"Hang on." Elias felt a little steadier now. "Sorry, I'm being a little slow." There was a rustle of fabric. "I snagged some potions from the lab the other day to try out. I think I've got a light potion here. Ah…"

He held up a tiny bottle and brilliant white light shone around the impromptu cave.

"Right then." He climbed to his feet. "Time to smash our way out."

"Elias, wait!" cried Nyree. "You can't just bash through. I'd have to drop the shield first. If I do the whole thing will collapse in on us."

Elias's face, still imp-blue turned a shade paler. "Sorry Nyree, I didn't think." He circled the small cave, slowly, looking for any detail that hinted at a way out. After a moment, he paused. "Hey, there's a flat bit here. I think it must be the wall."

"So, if we start digging at the other side," Nyree started.

"We should find a way out," finished Elias. "Can you shift the shield a little without dropping the whole thing?"

"In theory, yeah, but…" Nyree trailed off.

"Can you think of a better plan?

"Okay, okay, let's just do it." Nyree hissed. She frowned furiously for a moment, then said, "Ready?"

Elias settled in next to the first rock he planned to move. He nodded once. "Ready."

He felt an alarming flicker of magical energy, which quickly settled. His hands found the gap in the barrier, grasped the rock, and pulled. At first, nothing. Elias was about to suggest shifting the shield again and trying

164

elsewhere when he felt the stone move. He pulled it free creating a gap in the rubble. A trickle of dust filtered down, but the gap held.

"Alright, see? We'll be out in no time." Even to himself, Elias sounded unnatural and tense.

"Can you get another one, or should I widen the hole in the shield?" Nyree was shaking alarmingly. She took a breath. Then another and seemed to calm down.

"I think I can manage another…" Elias wrestled with the next one. "Ah, nuts." He groaned, leaning awkwardly into the hole. "Do you think you could slip the shield in here a bit and hold it open? I think I've dislodged something."

"Ha, nice one!" Nyree scoffed, then choked off abruptly. "Wait, you're serious?"

"Tiny bit, yeah." Elias grunted. It wasn't so much that the rubble was heavy, which it was, but the unhelpful position he had to occupy to hold it.

"You want the moon on a stick, you do." Nyree snatched two quick breaths, like a diver about to go under. Elias felt a trickle of power. The shield smoothly warped to hold up the gap.

Elias gave a strained chuckle as he shifted another block. "We should totally get the brownies to put a moon at the top of your staff."

Working this way, one dusty chunk of rock at a time, they made a sizable dent in the cave wall. Before long, there was something approaching a tunnel, which Elias needed to crawl through to pull out the stone.

At the end of one such trip, Nyree stopped him. "So,

I'm spotting a small problem here."

"Just the one?" quipped Elias. "Lucky us."

"We're kind of running out of space."

Elias looked around. The middle of the cave was getting crowded.

"Yeah, I was noticing that." Elias looked around again, surveying the remaining room. "I was basically hoping that we'd get out before we ran out of space, though."

"It doesn't look promising, does it?" said Nyree. "Actually," she added, brightening a bit, "couldn't you just eat the rocks? You've done it before."

"Do you have any idea how bad they taste?" Elias grimaced. "It'll take days to get rid of all the grit too. My dinner will be ruined."

"Beats missing it altogether though, doesn't it?"

Elias snorted slightly and turned to the tunnel once more. "Rock-cakes it is then," he sighed.

By the time they crawled out from under the ruined wall it was already late afternoon. As they dragged themselves into the sunlight, exhausted beyond words, there was a yell of delight from near the tower.

Feally ran over, his arms flailing wildly, "Thank goodness you two are alright!" Tears of relief were streaming down his face. "We were so worried. We've been trying to dig you out, but it seems we'd started in the wrong place. It was such slow going. So much stone – our magic wasn't able to clear it. We had to resort to brute force, which we just don't have much of. Oh, I'm so glad to see you both…"

"Okay, Feally," said Nyree soothingly, kneeling to hold him as if he were the one who had just escaped from a mound of rubble. "We're okay."

"Feally?" Elias interrupted. "Not to sound selfish or anything, but how come Mal isn't helping with the rescue?"

"Mal?" Feally looked around in confusion. "Oh, Malachite! Elias, I'm sorry, I don't know how to say this, but… He was taken."

"Taken?" said Elias and Nyree together.

"It was terrible." Feally studied his feet. "The goblins just kept piling up on him. He fought until the last, but when they finally brought him down, they had him. Smashed his legs with their wicked hammers. After that, they just dragged him off…" Feally's tears kept running.

"It's okay, Feally. Everything will be okay." Nyree wasn't convinced herself.

"They took my friend!" Feally's voice was an angry rip in the air. "They took him, and I did nothing!"

"What could you have done?" asked Elias. "You're not a fighter, and there were more than enough of the blighters to bring Malachite down. What could anyone possibly have done?"

"He fought alone." After his rage, Feally sounded weak, defeated. "He didn't have to fight alone. I should have stood by him and fought."

"And died?" Elias asked. "Would that have helped him?"

"If I canna fight for those I love, what's the point of me?" Feally barely whispered. "What's the point of me?"

"Oh, you can fight." A violent calm washed through Nyree. "We can all fight. We're not done yet. The goblins have taken our friend. We're getting him back."

She turned to Elias. "Can you see how much of a trail they've left? Don't go far, we just want to get an idea of what we're up against."

"No problem." Elias grinned and sprang away.

"Feally?" She turned back to the brownie. "We're going to need supplies. Food and shelter. Probably some rope. Anything else you can think of."

"Yes mistress!" Feally looked relieved at having some orders to follow. He turned to leave.

"One moment, Feally," said Nyree hastily. "Not done yet. Send someone to the library to find any maps of the area that look even remotely up to date or useful. Obviously if there's something with a big 'X' marked 'Goblin hideout here', that would be great, otherwise whatever we can get. Oh, and send someone to find out what's happened to Cauldron, please."

"Yes mistress!" Feally paused for a second. When it was clear that Nyree was actually finished this time, he scampered off.

Nyree turned around to survey the damage. The outer wall had been completely obliterated. The carefully formed masonry had been reduced to rubble for a full quarter arc around the gateway. The gate itself a tangle of metal just poking out from under the crumbling stone.

She started to sigh then abruptly stopped herself.

Grumbling didn't get things done. An idea started to form in Nyree's mind.

"You there," she called to the nearest brownie.

The brownie came running over. "Yes mistress?"

"Your clean-up magic. Can it restore broken things? Crockery and the like?"

"Yes, mistress," the brownie replied. She shuffled her feet and kept her eyes fixed on the grass.

"Please, look at me," Nyree said gently. "We're all friends here. Just trying to help each other, okay? And it's Nyree, alright? Just Nyree."

The brownie looked up, a nervous smile playing on her lips, "yes mistr... yes, Nyree."

"Now, what's your name?" Nyree forced herself to take her time. This needed to be done, however much she just wanted to rush off to find Malachite.

"I'm Meg Mullach, mis... Nyree."

"So, you can fix small things, but not big stuff like the wall?" Nyree pressed on to the matter in hand, she was forcing herself to take her time, not dawdle.

"Well, yeah. The wall is too big. We just don't have that kind of power. I've heard that it's because it's a glamour, but I don't really know about that stuff. All I know is that it works for household items, but not households, if you see what I mean."

"I do see." Nyree sounded pleased. "In fact, I was rather counting on that. I have an idea. Now please bear with me on this, could you try to use your power to fix the gateway?"

"Okay, I'll try," Meg's voice shook with worry, "but

don't expect much."

"It's just an idea." Nyree tried, mostly successfully, to sound casual. "It probably won't work, but we ought to try anyway."

Meg walked slowly over to the wreckage of the gateway and stopped by one of the smaller stones. She shot Nyree a nervous smile. "I'll start small, maybe I can do something at least."

Nyree smiled back and Meg stooped to place a hand on the rock. The rock shook slightly, as if it were trying to move back to its right place. Just as she seemed ready to give up, Nyree placed her hand gently on the brownies shoulder. Meg glanced questioningly at it. Nyree sent a gentle stream of power into the brownie.

Meg squealed in delight, then the air was filled with the sound of an avalanche. Every stone within ten metres of the gateway hurled itself into the air and smashed into its companions. Masonry re-fused into solid blocks and settled back into place with a sound like a mountain coming to rest. The metal of the gate screeched as it untwisted then leaped back into its mountings.

"That... was... incredible..." gasped Meg.

"Well, if you think you can manage a bit more," said Nyree with a smile, "we've got some work ahead of us."

Out of habit, Elias leaped to the top of the outer wall without so much as a glance. He felt a lurch of alarm in his gut, remembering that the wall had been destroyed. Then he landed atop clean, fresh stonework.

"Well, that was quick," he called down to Nyree, who was standing in the courtyard directing a bustle of activity.

"It wasn't really me." Nyree looked around, then gestured at the brownie standing next to her. "My new friend Meg did all the hard work. I just gave her a bit of a boost."

"The mistress…" Meg winced and glanced at Nyree. "Sorry, Nyree. Well, she's being too kind. Elias, your sister is completely amazing!"

"Okay, then." Elias filled his voice with sickly exasperation. He jumped down from the wall, rolled through the landing and stopped next to Nyree and Meg. "When you two are quite finished…" he looked at them expectantly.

"We should talk about the rebuilding work later." Nyree sounded excited. "I think you'll find it interesting. Anyway, what about the goblins? Any trace?"

"Not so much a trace." Elias shook his head. "More a map and set of sign-posts. It's like a herd of elephants driving bulldozers cleared a path for a stampede of rhinos." It was hard to believe the mess they'd made.

Nyree laughed at the image. "Okay, so you're telling me they'll be easy to follow, then."

"Yeah, I reckon we'll manage." Elias grinned. "How are the supplies coming along?"

"Pretty good, we've got the basics collected already. Food, water, ropes," Nyree pointed at a pair of stout looking back-packs.

"Shelter?"

"Feally and the other brownies are working on something at the moment." Nyree looked toward the tower. "Ah, here they come now."

Elias followed her gaze but saw no sign of any brownies anywhere. He was just about to ask his sister what she was talking about when the tower door opened, and a group of brownies bustled out. A brief glance confirmed that it was the same group which had given him the portable cauldron. Perhaps they were the engineering division.

"So, you're psychic now?" Elias tried hard not to be jealous of 'Awesome New Skill number one-hundred-and-seventy-two' or whatever his sister was up to now.

"Ha! No," Nyree's eyes crinkled with delight, "not psychic, exactly. I've been messing around with a perception spell. It helps me keep track of stuff I'm interested in near-by."

"What, like a spider-sense or something?" said Elias.

"You know that part never made sense to me." Cauldron popped up next to them, startling yelps out of Nyree, Elias and Meg. "In all my years, I've never met a spider who could see into the future."

"The rest of it is perfectly reasonable, of course?" Elias glamoured himself a look of unruffled calm, which he didn't feel at all.

"My dear boy. If a person was suddenly made like a spider, it surely follows quite naturally he would be the world's greatest super-hero, does it not?" Cauldron chuckled to himself. The sound sent shivers down Elias's spine. He was growing very fond of their potions master, however the sound of a giant spider laughing, especially quietly, was still deeply unsettling.

"Heh, okay." Elias managed to flatten the tremble in his voice.

"What's in the bag Cauldron?" Nyree gestured at the small silk sack that Cauldron was holding.

"I took the liberty of packing some potions and supplies which I thought you might find useful." Cauldron held the bag out to Nyree.

"Oh Cauldron, I could kiss you!" Reflexively Nyree stepped forward with her arms spread wide, then paused, as if unsure how to, or even if she should, proceed.

"An encounter which I think neither of us would enjoy, dear girl." Cauldron leaned back slightly and re-offered the bag of potions. "Our respective lips are somewhat incompatible, I'm afraid."

Nyree stepped back, a slight flush showing on her cheeks. "Well, if thoughts count for anything..."

"Everything my dear," said Cauldron. "In this, as in all things, they count for everything."

Feally, who had been waiting for attention, finally gave a slight cough, "Master, Mistress? We've made you a tent."

He held out a small brown cube, the size of an orange. As Nyree was about to take it, Elias snatched it up and began peering closely at its surface, earning him a glare from his big sister.

"Let me guess." He grinned at Feally. "You've tidied this up too?"

"Why yes, Master, I did. It may be my only trick, but

I flatter myself that it is a rather good one. If you would care to inspect it, it may be opened by squeezing it gently in your bare hand."

Elias gave the cube a squeeze and to his surprise the surface pushed back, forcing his hand open. He dropped it quickly, which turned out to be the right thing to do. As it hit the ground, the cube performed a series of complicated unfoldings before popping up into its final shape and size.

"Wow!" Nyree jumped out of the way of the expanding canvas.

Elias eyed Feally with a new respect and some interest. The brownies were able to contort their seemingly limited magic in unexpected and powerful ways. He'd have to look into this once things settled down.

The 'tent' was huge. More a grand royal pavilion, in Elias's opinion. Like something from a King Arthur movie.

"To your liking, I hope?" Feally did a terrible job of hiding his pride.

Elias stepped through the tent flap to have a look around.

"Cool!" he called out. "It's even got a fully set dining table. We've got a room each, and a couple of spares."

"Nice." Nyree was grinning as she and Feally stepped inside. "One thing, though. How do we put it away again?"

"You see that rope there?" Feally gestured at what looked surprisingly like a bell pull. "Give it a tug with your bare hand, and the tent will fold itself back up into its transport cube. Try not to be inside when it does."

"Thank you again Feally." Nyree picked him up in a hug. "Brilliant, as ever."

With the packing completed, Elias slung his backpack onto his shoulders.

Nyree called over to him. "One last thing." She pulled out her phone, biting her lip as she did so. "We need to call Dad."

"And tell him what exactly?" If Elias's eyebrows could be raised further, it wasn't clear how. "Are you really going to ask permission to wander off into the wilderness after a band of armed goblins in search of our kidnapped magic teacher?"

"No, I suppose I probably shouldn't tell him that." Nyree frowned. "We could tell him that we're staying at Amy's house."

"Who?"

"Amy Fowler," said Nyree. "She's a girl in my class. We got on okay before the end of term."

"So, you've known her for like, two weeks."

"Yeah, but she seems nice. Can you believe, she's a 'Chalet School' fan! I mean, what are the chances?" Nyree noticed Elias rolling his eyes at this and hastily added, "She's into rock-climbing too, though. You'd probably like her."

"Alright, but do you know her well enough for us both to stay at her house?"

Nyree stared in disbelief at her brother. "You know we're not actually doing that, right?"

"I meant: is it believable? Anyway, won't Dad want to speak to her mum?" Elias snapped back. "Besides, when did you become so comfortable with lying to Dad?"

"Like you say, we can't tell him the truth. Also, yes, he will want to speak to one of her parents. If only we knew someone who could make things seem different to how they really are."

"You're really okay with using magic to lie to Dad?"

"If we're going to lie, and I can't think of any other alternative, we should at least do it well." Nyree sighed, "I wish we didn't have to, I really do, but I'm out of ideas."

Elias frowned. "Nope, I've got nothing either. Okay, call him."

Nyree tapped the 'home' shortcut, took a deep breath, and held the phone to her ear.

Chapter 18

The Search

Elias hadn't been exaggerating. The goblins' trail through the woods was a mess. Bushes and even small trees had been hacked down and flattened underfoot, leaving a path of trodden earth ten metres across.

Elias broke the uncomfortable silence after twenty awkward minutes. "You had to do it you know, there was no way around it."

Nyree sighed. "I know, I know. But I hate lying to Dad."

"Do you think he suspects?"

She didn't. They had lied well. Nyree kept her gaze clamped firmly to the floor. She couldn't bring herself to meet Elias's eyes. "That's the worst part of it. It's one thing trying your luck, but this…"

"Pretty rubbish of us, really."

"Not helping!" Irritating was in the little brother job

description, but Nyree sometimes wished he was a little less good at it.

"No, sorry, I suppose not." Elias paused for a moment. "What else could you do, though? I mean the truth just isn't an option at all. You couldn't just not call. Imagine what would happen when we didn't get home for dinner?"

"Good grief, he'd be furious!" Nyree glanced at her brother.

"And then what? You'd either have to lie then or stop answering his calls completely." Elias paused again, letting it sink in, "And then... well you know what Dad's like."

Nyree laughed at that. Couldn't help herself. "One-man task force! He'd probably set up some kind of signal tracking on our phones, grab a bunch of supplies and head off into the wilderness to rescue us. Odds are Mum would find him wandering in circles in the woods at around midnight, either in tears or beyond furious!"

"The apple doesn't fall far from the tree, does it?" Elias gave her a smirk, "Lucky this trail is so utterly unmissable."

"Hey! I'm not that..." Nyree stopped dead. Dread realisation chilled her. "I'm such an idiot!"

"Just like Dad." Elias grinned. "All I'm saying."

"No, shush a moment." Nyree cocked her head, listening intently. "If I were the goblins, the only way I'd leave a trail like this one is if I wanted it to be followed. That way I'd be sure of exactly where my pursuers were coming from and could pick a spot for an ambush."

"Yeah, but they aren't you." Elias looked

unimpressed. "I mean, goblins are supposed to be cave dwelling, knuckle-dragging imbeciles."

"Says who? Tolkien?" Nyree was kneeling now, looking at the trail more closely. "How many goblins do you think he actually met? Even if he had, we already know that faerie folk can be as different as different gets. What's to say that goblins aren't really clever little creatures?"

"Alright, calm down." Elias looked thoughtful now too. "You could be right. I guess it won't hurt too much to get off the trail for a while and see."

"I have a better idea." Nyree slipped her staff out of the hastily constructed holder on her backpack. "Grab on."

Nyree and Elias flew a little above the treetops. High enough that they were clear of the upper foliage, but not so high that they would miss any signs of the goblins.

A mile ahead, where the path turned beneath a small cliff face, they saw it. A small group of goblins had rigged a rockslide from above. Archers lurked opposite the cliff-face. Nyree counted half a dozen goblins further down the trail, and Elias claimed that he could smell a bunch more hiding in the bushes a little way back. Nyree and Elias landed in a nearby clearing to consider what to do.

"You know, we could just go past them." Elias sat on a rock and poked at the soil with a stick.

"Yeah, but then we'd have the wee gits behind us as well as in front." Nyree sat opposite on a tree-stump idly bouncing the end of her staff off her toes. "I think we need to deal with them."

"I'm pretty sure we can take them." Elias sounded fed-up. "I mean, we've got the element of surprise, and we're not exactly helpless. I just…"

"Yeah, I don't really feel like fighting either." Nyree rested her staff on her head. Deep down she still worried that it wasn't really the goblins' fault. "I just wish I could think of a way to keep them here for a bit. I'd tie them up, but I don't reckon they'll come quietly."

"Oooh! I've got an idea." Elias sat up sharply and rummaged in his pack for his portable cauldron.

Elias crept through the undergrowth toward the archers. He didn't really need to sneak. He'd put on a glamour to mask any sounds and make himself invisible. Still, he liked to feel stealthy. For his own satisfaction if nothing else. This was the key part of the plan. Nyree was going to fly past the rockslide operators at the top of the cliff and dowse them with potion before they could respond. With all the tree cover down here though, that wasn't an option for the archers. Once they were dealt with, the ground troops shouldn't be too much of a problem. So here he was, sneaking through the woods to hit each of the archers in turn with his slow-down potion. The good thing was, unless he messed up, his victims wouldn't be able to make a sound for quite some while. Unless he messed up. Not that he expected to, of course, the goblins were all basically sitting targets who had no idea that he was there.

His glamour would protect him from detection even if he wasn't being sneaky.

He slid up to the first goblin, who was hiding in a bush and watching the road intently. Elias hesitated for a moment, then slipped the stopper from the potion bottle and poured a sizable dose over his target. The goblin didn't even stir before the potion took effect.

One down, three more to go, Elias nodded to himself and crept onward.

The next was sitting in a tree just before the bend at the core of the trap. With a quick leap and a couple of smooth, practiced movements Elias hung by his legs from the branch above the would-be ambusher. The leaves hadn't even shivered. Another stopper, another large dose of potion.

Based on his previous experiments, Elias had brewed the potion and planned the doses to give them about a day before it would wear off. Then he doubled it. No sense in going easy on the goblins, just because he didn't want to hurt them.

Elias slipped in behind the third goblin. Confident by now, he stood up, opened the third bottle, and poured.

"Hey!" The rasping voice of the final archer scoured the clearing between its owner and Elias.

Astonishment froze Elias to the spot. He didn't understand what could have gone wrong. Footsteps rushed from both directions along the path. Half a breath later Elias recovered his wits. He leap-frogged the now frozen goblin and flung the last dose of potion, bottle and all, at the final archer. The bottle hit the goblin's helmet on a row of outward pointing spikes, showering the hapless creature with slow-motion-potion. Elias landed, rolling sideways to avoid any stray splashes and sprang to his feet on the trail.

"Elias! Move!" Nyree yelled from somewhere above.

He dived back into the trees, grabbed a low branch and swung for cover. His hiding place in the undergrowth offered a clear view of the path. Goblins charged in from both sides. They turned toward the forest where Elias was hiding. Magical sparks exploded directly above the goblins. Potion rained on the entire squad of goblin soldiers locking them in place.

Nyree swooped in through the trees, landing clumsily next to Elias. "Well that nearly got away from us!" She grinned wildly at her brother. "What happened?"

"Don't know," said Elias. "The last archer happened to be looking my way. I should have been invisible though, so I don't…" He slapped his forehead in annoyance. "Of course, I didn't think to glamour the potion. He must have seen it pouring."

"Oops." Nyree chuckled. "Well, we got away with it, anyway. Shall we go?"

It was getting dark when Nyree and Elias reached the edge of the woods. Beyond the trees the trail became harder to follow until, finally, it vanished among the heather covered hills.

Nyree lifted herself a few metres into the air and flew slowly around searching for any signs.

"I think we've lost them." Nyree sank to the ground. "Any signs down here?"

"Nope." Elias was still hunched over, scurrying back and forth searching for any clues. "Can't really see much anymore, though."

"Would some light help?" Nyree held up her staff and a bright white light flared from its top.

"Nah, it's just casting shadows all over the place." Elias straightened up scowling at the summer twilight. "Give up for the night?"

"Seems about right." Nyree sighed heavily. "Even if we knew where they went, I guess we should get some rest anyway. I hate losing so much time, though."

Elias shuddered as he looked at the wide-open grasslands all around him. "Can we find something a bit less in the open?"

"There's a wee hillock over there," Nyree pointed broadly in the direction they had been heading, "and a stream next to it. Seems like as good a place to camp as any."

Setting up camp was far easier than they remembered. Of course, they didn't have a magic tent and sorcery the last time. On their previous trips, heat and light had been delivered by some comfortless blue-white LED lamps and a half-hearted campfire.

"Do you remember Dad battling with that tent in the middle of the night?" Elias chuckled as he stirred the soup bubbling in his cauldron.

"You mean the one in Pitlochry?" Nyree grinned back.

"No, before that. You remember, when Dad had that daft notion to take us all on an overnight ramble through Rannoch moors?"

"Oh, goodness, I'd forgotten. That orange monstrosity that had all the wrong poles and everything." Nyree chuckled at the memory.

"I actually felt pretty sorry for Dad lugging the thing about all day only to find that it couldn't actually be built."

"You'd think he'd have thought to test it first though."

"What? Our dad?" Elias looked genuinely puzzled.

"No, you're right," Nyree mused, "Mum would though. I wonder why she didn't make him check it before the trip."

"Ran out of time I guess." Elias rummaged in his backpack for some bowls. "You know how they are with their grand schemes – never quite get around to half of them."

"Nice that they try though. Thanks," Nyree took the offered bowl from Elias. She blew on a spoonful and had a sip. "Oh, this is nice. When'd you learn to make this?"

Elias raised an eyebrow at his sister. "You know I've been helping Dad make dinner for ages."

"Well, yeah." Nyree shrugged. "I just didn't think you actually did that much."

Elias snorted. "Thanks, sis. Good to be appreciated."

"No, I just…" Nyree bit her lip. "Sorry."

They ate in silence for a few moments before Nyree tried to pick up their earlier conversation.

"You do have to hand it to Dad though – it was a

pretty impressive bit of improvisation, hacking that tent into something you could actually sleep under."

"True. But then that's Dad in his element isn't it. I wonder what they're up to just now." Elias looked a little bit lost and alone, beneath a bold façade.

"Well, Mum's out at choir." Nyree blew on another spoonful of soup. "Dad is probably tinkering about with some project or other. Hopefully, he'll have remembered to have dinner."

A quiet snigger from Elias. "Yeah, something crazy like— hey what was that?"

They both sat silent. As still as bricks. Straining to hear the slightest noise. They were about to relax, then they heard it again. Sobbing. Almost certainly. Nyree lifted a finger to her lips and reached with her other hand for her staff. Elias nodded, then closed his eyes, concentrating for a moment.

"Okay." He stood and stepped over to Nyree. "I've hidden us and projected fakes where we were. We should be able to sneak up on whatever that is."

Nyree nodded, not quite trusting to her brother's glamour to hide her voice. She glanced over her shoulder to where their decoys sat and had to stifle a cry of surprise. "Dear goodness, that's creepy!" Her voice rasped with shock as she whispered to Elias.

"Good, isn't it?" Elias grinned back at her. "Let's go see what's out there."

They slipped out of the tent and toward the stream, which seemed to be where the sound was coming from. As their eyes adjusted to the dark, they could make out the shape of someone facing away from them at the water's edge. Judging from the shoulder movements the person was crying.

"It could be a trap." Nyree whispered.

The figure sat up sharply, the sobbing sound stopping abruptly. Its head turned and just at that moment, the moon slipped out from behind a cloud its light revealing the face of a young woman. She had a pleasant, kindly face. The sort you wouldn't run away from in a playground or park. As Mum would say, the kind of face shared by saints and psychopaths. It was streaked with tears, which glistened in the moonlight. After the longest, stillest moment, the woman turned back to the stream and continued in her grief.

Nyree nodded to Elias, then drew herself up. She'd been half crouching since leaving the tent. "Hello there," she called to the woman as Elias dropped the stealth glamour. "Are you okay?"

"Aye lass, I will be." The woman's otherworldly voice floated back through the night.

Nyree approached, her caution held in balance between the woman's obvious distress and the sudden appearance of a stranger. Right next to their camp. In the middle of nowhere. And at night. As they drew closer, they could see that she was washing clothes. Bloodstained clothes.

Nyree's gaze was drawn to the clothes. It was like when someone drops a plate in the school lunch-hall. Looking away didn't seem to be possible. There was something hypnotic about them. An unshakable eerie

186

feeling.

A quick glance at her brother confirmed, Elias saw it too. The colours, the size, even the style. They could almost be Elias's clothes. With a gasp, Nyree realised who — what — this was.

"A banshee," she whispered with a strained squeak in her voice.

"You mean, like, the ones that scream at you and then you..." A stern look from his sister cut Elias off.

"What brings you two out here, all alone in the middle of the night I wonder?" the banshee's voice was smooth as silk and as inviting as a noose.

"We're..." Nyree ended in another squeak of nerves, recovered then tried again, "We're Nyree and Elias Forester. We're looking for our friend who was taken by goblins. Please, have you seen any sign of them? We've, sort of, lost the trail."

Elias stood silently now. His gaze fixed intensely on the clothes that the banshee was washing.

"You are the ones I was sent to find." The banshee had stopped her futile washing now and turned her heart-riven eyes to Nyree. "I bring a message from the great Unseelie Court. A message and a warning."

Questions buzzed in Nyree's mind. What was the message? Who were the *Un*seelie Court? Where had the goblins gone? All these were driven from her mind by a rising dread for the warning.

"Please, before you go on," Nyree was shaking now, and it had nothing to do with the cool night air, "I've read that a visit from a banshee was an omen of death in the family…" She trailed off, unable to say out loud what worried her most.

"Those are my clothes," Elias mumbled, his face white as a ghost. "I die tomorrow, don't I?"

"The legends aren't true." The banshee smiled sadly at them. "Not entirely, at least. Indeed, I come to foretell death. But it is not a fixed future I see. Instead, I see the shadows of all possibilities.

"Nyree, tomorrow your brother will be in mortal danger and he will die because you love him. When the time comes, you will face a choice. Choose wrongly and he will certainly perish. Then all will be lost. This was the warning I was sent to bring."

"What choice?" Panicked hysteria started to overwhelm Nyree. "What danger? Tell me more? What choice? Tell me please! What should I do?"

"And I suppose I can't do anything." Elias sounded angry now. "I'm not exactly helpless you know!"

"I'm sorry Elias." The banshee seemed genuinely saddened. "That much is clear. Your actions can neither lessen the peril, nor make certain your fate."

"But—" Nyree wanted to argue, to deny the banshee's warning, to shake a different future from her.

"Hush, child." The banshee put a finger to her lips. It was like the air had been sucked out of Nyree's lungs. "More on this I cannot say. Hear now my message from the great Unseelie Court. The goblins are not acting on our behalf. Had we predicted their treachery, we would have prevented their foul deeds most decisively. A guide from among our lesser minions has been dispatched to you and will arrive tomorrow. Go with the blessings of the great Unseelie Court. Farewell."

The banshee faded from sight, her voice drifting to silence like a summer breeze.

Nyree awoke to pale light glowing through the tent. Morning, but still early. She groaned quietly. Not a good night's sleep. The most awful dreams had hounded her, circling back to hundreds of scenarios that ended with a dead brother. Elias! She couldn't imagine what it must be like for him. She peeled herself grudgingly out of bed. At least she could make him a decent breakfast.

A sound made her freeze in place. Then nothing. Silence rang in her ears. Imagination? No, there it was again. Soft, wet sniffing. Muffled, trying hard not to be heard, but definitely there. Just outside the tent.

Nyree parted the flaps and crept out of her bedroom. Maybe she could surprise whatever was sneaking up on them. What she saw tore at her heart more than any anticipated horror.

Elias sat just outside the tent, bathed eerily in the predawn grim-light. He hunched over something in his lap. A tear fell from his cheek and landed, plock, on something hard. Plastic or glass.

Nyree darted back into her bedroom, taking care to rustle the fabric. She yawned loudly and stepped out clattering into the pile of last night's plates, which had cleaned themselves. Brownie magic again. Nyree stole a moment to smile. It might be her last chance for a while.

She looked up in time to see Elias hurriedly wiping his eyes. He jumped up and turned to her. Big-sister mode kicked in as she noticed his hand slip quickly behind his back and stay there.

Nyree's brow clenched as she asked, "What're you hiding?"

"Nothing, I—" Elias sighed. He brought his hand forward and held out Nyree's phone. The screen showed their dad's contact page. "I just really wanted to talk to him, you know."

"I know." Nyree stepped over and hugged her brother tightly. "You know we can't though."

"Obviously." Elias pushed Nyree away and stepped back, rolling his eyes theatrically. "Can you imagine that conversation? Hi Dad. So, yesterday we were lying. We've run off into the woods and put ourselves in mortal danger. Nyree should be back later, but I'm probably going to..." He trailed off. Nyree reached for him but stopped when determination claimed her brothers face. "I'm going to keep you safe though. That's for sure."

"You're what?" That wasn't what Nyree expected.

"Well," Elias flashed a too-tight grin at her, "the banshee said nothing I do can change it. Which means, basically that I'm invincible, until... you know."

"That's not what that means at all!" shrieked Nyree. "What kind of muddle-minded boy-logic is that? Of all the stupid... I mean, really!"

"It's not stupid. It makes perfect sense."

"No," Nyree yelled back at him. "You keep yourself

safe. You take care of that."

"But that's the point." Elias was being unreasonably reasonable now. It made Nyree want to punch him. "What if I run? Maybe that's the opening they need. Do you follow? Do you press on with the rescue? Is that the choice that saves me? So, I make myself invisible. They can't ki— hurt what they can't see right? What if they shoot at you and I just happen to be in the way? What if the decision that saves me is you telling me not to be so stupid and just be visible? What about that? What if…"

"I know!" Nyree wanted to grab Elias and shake him. She wanted to hug him and tell him it would all be okay. He was right. Of course he was right. That didn't make it acceptable. The whole thing was just too horrible to wrap her head around. And her brother's safety lay on her shoulders. "Just don't take any stupid risks, okay?"

"Like letting something ugly sneak up behind you?" A new voice. Alarmingly close.

Elias spun into a low crouch, his skin flashing to bright battle-blue. The magic staff burst through the tent flaps and snapped into Nyree's left hand. An eyeblink later a fireball formed in her right.

A small man stood among the tufts of long yellowing grass. Little larger than a brownie but stocky and solidly built. His skin was a grey brown with grizzled, mousey hair sticking out in every direction.

"Aaagh!" The creature screamed, then dived for the grass and disappeared into a small mound.

"Please don't hurt me." This time its voice was muffled. "I was sent by the court to be your guide."

Nyree put out the fireball. She tried to shrug some tension from her shoulders. "Okay. We won't hurt you. Just, now isn't really a good time to startle us."

The creature emerged cautiously. Seeing Elias, still blue and ready for a fight, it very carefully took a couple of extra steps away.

"Well?" Elias stepped forward. "Who and what are you? How can you help us? Quickly, I'm not feeling patient today."

The creature stammered, stepped back, and tripped on a tussock of grass. It staggered but kept its feet. "I'm Perjink and I'm just a wee trow. I know exactly who the goblins are and where they've gone. I'll lead you to them, I promise, just please don't hurt me!"

"Elias, back off, he's trying to help." Nyree held her hand out to Elias, who looked like he might ignore her.

Elias abruptly stopped. He sagged as his blue hue and anger drained away.

"Sorry," he said softly. "I'm just wound a bit tight this morning. You know, last day and all." Elias tried a grim chuckle, but it came out tense and false.

"I heard about that." Perjink straightened his clothes. "Those foul renegades think they can put an end to you, but they won't, I know it. The Court knows it too, or they wouldn't have sent me. Oh no, they'd have sent someone powerful that could stop 'em. See, you two are important to the Court, even I can see that."

"Sorry, what?" Nyree crouched down in front of Perjink. "Renegades?"

"Aye," Perjink nodded. "Oh, sorry, you don't know,

do you? The goblins are renegades, traitors to the Court. About three weeks ago they were fine. As grand a bunch of mischief-makers as you could hope for. Then suddenly," he snapped his fingers, "they just went mad. Renounced the Court and recanted their blood-oaths. Unbelievably, the queen says we can't act against them. Something about raising an ancient evil before its time. Didn't make much sense to be honest. I'd have thought she'd be furious."

"So, you know where they are then?" Elias was eager to get going. Hanging around waiting for his doom was worse than attacking it with the fury it deserved.

"Aye, that I do." Perjink gestured vaguely over his shoulder, "There's an old quarry a few hours walk over that way. Can't see it without knowing, but there's a cave hidden in it that's the entrance to their lair."

"You were sent by the Seelie Court? I wonder why they didn't send Faltha instead." Nyree had turned, looking back in the direction of the tower. Not that she could have seen it from here. They were a long way from any other help.

"Seelie Court! How dare you!" screamed Perjink. "And as for that flighty wee frippet, Faltha! Ha! For all that I'm not much use, she'd be worse. Probably get you both killed into the bargain, and I'm not saying by accident either."

"Sorry," said Nyree hastily. "I thought you said… hang on. There's more than one faery court?"

"Good grief, you two really are green, aren't you?" Perjink drew himself up, though it had precious little effect. "There are two courts of the faery folk in these parts. The Great Unseelie Court, and the Seelie Court. Now, Unseelie is the true court of all free-thinking faerie folk. It fosters creativity among its people and invites us to use our gifts in whatever way takes our fancy. Those stuck-up, self-important Seelie's on the other hand. Well, they're all about rules. They don't mind what you do, so long as it's exactly what they say. Foul bunch they are."

"Faltha's a friend of ours and has always been a good one." Elias glowered at Perjink. His imp-blue highlighted his dark eyes menacingly. "If you don't like her, that looks bad on you."

"Elias, stop that," Nyree snapped. "Perjink is here to help us. Whatever faery court politics is going on can wait. We've got to rescue Malachite. We can deal with the rest later."

"Fine then." Elias didn't ease his scowl. "Lead on then trow."

Perjink, now looking thoroughly cowed by Elias, turned in the direction he'd indicated. "This way," he mumbled as he trudged off through the grass.

"Oh, for goodness' sake." Nyree muttered, rolling her eyes. She snatched up her staff, grabbed Perjink by the arm and took to the air.

"Hang on." Elias headed back to the tent. "What about the camp?"

"Good point. We might want some of that stuff." Nyree circled back with Perjink hanging rather indignantly below her.

"Alright, give me a moment." Elias vanished into the tent for a moment, then emerged carrying their two packs.

He jerked on the rope to magically fold and compress the tent. Stuffing the tent-cube in his pack he slung it over his shoulder and with barely a glance leaped the three metres up to the staff. He grabbed on with his free hand, sat down and rode like a witch on a broom.

"Comfy there?" asked Nyree with a grin.

"I'll live." Elias grinned wildly back to her.

"Hope so little brother." Nyree said quietly. The sound was lost in the wind as they flew toward the goblins cave and their moment of reckoning.

Chapter 19

Prisoners

They flew in silence. Perjink guided them with occasional gestures and, too soon, they reached the quarry. It had clearly been abandoned as an active work site a long time ago. All that was left was a horseshoe cliff facing roughly north-west, ideal for catching the evening sun, but decidedly chilly in the early morning. The cliff looked out over a broken, rocky grassland covered in gorse bushes and surrounded by loose forest.

Nyree landed them a little way back from the treeline, directly facing the cliff in a slightly denser patch of woodland. They settled into the scant cover to plan their approach.

"Here we are then." Perjink waved proudly at the quarry. "The Faerykirk. Currently the home of everyone's least favourite band of renegade goblins. If you look closely, you'll see the entrance there on the left. That extra shadowy bit at the bottom that you can't quite focus on. I'm told, that's the leftovers of some ancient faery magic designed to hide the gate. This used to be the home of the great Unseelie Court."

"Oh, yeah, I see it." Elias peered at the shaded cliff face for a moment, "So what's the plan sis? Full on assault, or do you have something better planned?"

"I was thinking about it on the way over." Nyree studied the rock-face as she spoke, "It seems to me that attacking them could get messy pretty quickly. We don't know where Malachite is being held, nor anything about what's inside. There's a couple of sentries further up the cliff face. They seem to be asleep or something. Don't seem to have noticed us yet anyway."

"Okay." The patience in Elias's voice had a distinctly forced edge to it. "So, what is the plan?"

"Oh, it's a good one," replied Nyree, "but you're not going to like it at all."

◦◦◦◦◦

The trio strolled across the quarry floor, directly for the hidden entrance. They didn't even make the slightest effort toward stealth. Nyree led the way, striding confidently, a big smile fixed firmly on her face. Behind her stalked Elias, his barely contained rage adding a menace to his stride.

Following further behind, and much less boldly, was Perjink. His listless gaze was flitting from shadow to bush, as if ambush might come at any moment.

"You know, you really could have stayed behind, Perjink." Nyree's words echoed off the cliffs, seeming to fill the whole space with their cheery lilt. "You've done your part. You really don't need to come with us."

"No." Perjink sounded nervous, twitchy, and even smaller than usual. "I really think I need to see this through. Besides, they know my name now. Thanks for that, by the way. If this goes badly, I very much doubt that I'd escape them, anyway. Goblins can hold a grudge like nothing else on Earth."

"I still can't believe that your great plan is to knock on the door and ask for Malachite back." Elias's expression was a balancing act between incredulity at his sister's plan, fury at the goblins, and his dread of what might follow.

"Well," Nyree grinned, "diplomacy is always worth a shot."

"Yeah, if you have something to bargain with." Elias glowered at the door as if he could wrench it from its mounting with a look. "We even left most of our stuff back there under a bush."

"Really?" Surprise stopped Nyree in her tracks. She stared at her brother in astonishment. "You don't think we have any bargaining tools? Well, I'm quite disappointed you see it that way."

Stunned silence followed. Nyree continued her march up to the gates of Faerykirk and thumped twice on the door with her fist. The sound jolted Elias into action. He sprang forward to take his place next to Nyree. However daft her plan seemed to him he wasn't going to

199

abandon her for anything.

"What is it?" an irritable, spiky voice demanded from within.

"I am Nyree, and this is my brother Elias. We're here to negotiate for the release of your prisoner Malachite."

"Foolish girl." The voice behind the door cackled. "We will never release him. Get them!"

Even as he spoke, the ground around them erupted. A dozen goblins burst out of their hiding places among the rocks and bushes. Each was armed with an evil looking spear, which they brandished with a well-practiced ease.

It was only a brief glimpse of the goblins. A huge sack -like canvas was shot from above, engulfing Nyree, Elias and Perjink in darkness.

The cell door slammed with a clang and a smooth click. Elias burst out from under the canvas. He landed shimmering blue in the dimness of the goblins' dungeons, wearing an expression that threatened pain and destruction to anything in his way.

Far more calmly, but somehow less gracefully, Nyree emerged from the sack. She was grinning widely. She held up her hand, conjured a sorcerous light and floated it up to the ceiling.

"Well, this is not what I was expecting at all." Nyree turned around slowly, taking in the small cell.

It was far from the damp, rotting, shambles of a room suggested by all the stories. Instead, they were in an extremely well-maintained little chamber. The walls were smooth stone, polished to a shine. The bars at the front were of gleaming metal, clean and well looked-after. Even the bed was nicely made up. Nyree half expected a little mint on the pillow.

"Well, I'm glad you like our cell!" Elias paced back and forth near the bars. "Our so-called rescue mission is done before it's even started. Negotiate! Brilliant idea sis."

"Elias? Nyree? Is that you?" came a familiar voice from the next cell.

"Hi, Malachite." Nyree replied. She looked entirely un-surprised. "We're both here to rescue you."

"Hang on." Elias abruptly stopped his pacing and whipped around to stare at his sister. "This was the plan?"

"Yup." Nyree beamed at her brother. "Figured the easiest way to find a prisoner was to become one. I paid attention on the way in. I think I can lead us out again. Just got to get out of here first."

"You think?" muttered Elias.

"Children." Malachite's voice cracked with emotion. "I thought you were dead. When I saw the wall collapse, I was sure it was all over. I just... I'm just..."

"I know Malachite. It's okay. I kinda thought that too, for a bit," said Nyree. "We're fine though. It's going to be fine."

"Well," added Elias, "except that we're all still prisoners of the goblins. Apparently in the luxury cell-block"

"Actually, all their cells are like this." Perjink had finally managed to free himself from the sack. "There's nothing the goblins take more seriously than hostages. You see, a squalid cell is weak. Crumbling stone, rusty iron, broken old beds, these are all a great help to a would-be-escapee. Now, see this bed? Notice how it's built into the walls. So, there's no using it to break your way out, nor any chance of using it as a weapon. The bars are dwarf steel. They'll never bend or break except by the hand that forged them."

"Right, so inescapable prison then." Elias was sitting comfortably on the bed now, and back to his human colour. "What's the plan sis?"

"Well," Nyree sounded calm and confident. Thoroughly in control. "I've been practicing lock-opening spells recently."

Elias shook his head slightly. "What on earth made you think of that?"

"I was really just curious." Nyree laughed as she walked to the door. "Anyway, time to open this... Oh."

"What?" Elias hopped off the bed. His smile faded.

"Umm... there's..." Nyree bit her lip. "There's, kind of, no lock."

"So, there you go then?" Elias looked confused.

Nyree shoved the door, on the off chance. "Nope, won't budge."

"Powrie Lock." Malachite pressed his head against the bars of his own cell. "It's magic woven by the ancient goblin clan, the Powries. As I understand it, these doors can only be opened by the being who closed them."

Nyree slumped to the floor. "Well, I wish I'd known that half-an-hour ago."

"So, what now then?" Elias looked on, unbelieving that Nyree didn't know what to do next.

Nyree sat in a trance. She'd projected her mind out of the prison and through to the guard chamber at the end of the corridor. She hoped to find out something that could help them. With her magical sight, she could see one guard on duty, sitting with his feet up at a small desk. Naturally, with the perfect prison, there was no need for vigilance.

"You could try a mind control spell." Malachite's voice snapped her attention back into her cell.

"That's a bit dark side, isn't it?" Nyree leaned against the cell-door, as if ideas for defeating the lock would filter through the bars and into her head.

"It's not ideal, certainly," Malachite rumbled quietly.

"I mean, some of your possible soul-stealers did that kind of stuff."

"True enough, but I seem to have run out of other options."

"Malachite?" Nyree sat up, "Do you think that was what the prophecy meant? That we'd try using the enemy's tactics and end up even worse than they are?"

"I don't know, Nyree," sighed Malachite. "At the moment, though, I fear that the prophecy is somewhat irrelevant if we remain stuck in this cage."

"Fair enough," agreed Nyree. "What do I need to do?"

"Well, it's rather challenging at the best of times, and

you have to see your target. Still, I do believe it is worth the attempt."

Malachite and Nyree settled into their usual teacher and pupil routine as Malachite explained the spell. It was indeed quite complicated magic, even without the added consideration of the mind-walking, which Nyree would have to do at the same time in order to see the goblin guard.

Elias and Perjink were helping by keeping out of the way. Elias had used a glamour to create a virtual chess board. He and Perjink were now deeply engrossed in their game, although Elias didn't seem to be meeting much resistance. Perjink was, at best, a sloppy player.

The four were so enthralled by their activities that they almost didn't notice the quiet clang and thump from the guard room. Nyree looked up as its door swung open. Elias leaped across the cell, landing battle ready and blue next to his sister.

Faltha flittered excitedly into the prison corridor.

"Well, hello you lot," she giggled. "Fancy meeting you here."

"Faltha!" Nyree and Elias said together. "You're here!"

"How?" asked Nyree.

At the same moment, Elias asked: "Why?"

"Glamour and rebellion," Faltha settled on the bars, her wings still fluttering rapidly. "Obviously, I couldn't have numpty out there and his even-thicker friends seeing me. I managed to sneak in past them all. It took a while to find the guard chamber and get in here, so, sorry I'm late.

As for the why. I wanted to help, obviously. The court told me I couldn't meddle because these are 'events of prophecy' or some such nonsense. But I figured that it's not like fate can be broken by little old me. So here I am. Oh, one moment…"

Faltha flew away again, back to the guard room. A moment later she came back, slower this time, dragging the unconscious guard. She hauled his hand up to the door of Malachite's cell and held it against the bars. Malachite pushed, and the door slid smoothly open with the faintest snick.

"Malachite, I'm glad to see you're okay." Faltha smiled weakly at him.

"Why Faltha," Malachite's warm growl sounded surprised, "I didn't know you cared."

"Well, they do," Faltha nodded sideways toward Nyree's and Elias's cell, "so I do."

Malachite dragged the goblin guard by the hand to the next cell and used it, perhaps more roughly than necessary, to open the door. As Nyree, Elias and Perjink stepped out, Malachite threw the guard in and moved to close the door. Nyree grabbed his wrist.

"Don't," she pleaded. "He'll be stuck in there forever. Malachite, please, don't make this worse."

"Mistress," Malachite growled. His fist clenched on the door-bars, and for a moment Nyree thought he was going to close it anyway. Then he turned and with the others stalked from the jail.

Chapter 20

Escape

Faltha led the way through the twisting warrens of passageways which made up the lower part of the goblin stronghold. Nyree had memorised the route on the way in, as part of her escape plan. Despite this, it was a relief to let Faltha guide them. Now that leading was someone else's problem, Nyree was free to see the goblins' lair.

They were not the dank, darksome caves described in stories. The word 'cave' hardly seemed fitting at all for the glorious halls they were now escaping. Bright paintings and beautiful, intricate carvings adorned the walls. Everywhere was lit by spheres of magical light held up by delicate smoky glass sconces.

Perjink had said that this was once the seat of the Unseelie Court, so Nyree almost dismissed its beauty as the works of the previous tenants, crediting the goblins with merely not wrecking the place. A closer look at a few paintings dispelled that illusion. Each one depicted goblin heroes in the throes of enacting some mischief or other.

As they were nearing the great-hall, one painting caught Nyree's eye. It showed a huge humanoid creature, a giant or such-like, crashing to the ground. On the giant's back was a single goblin, cackling manically and pointing at the giant's feet. Delighting in his cleverness, apparently, of tying the giant's shoelaces together. A nearby band of delighted goblins rolled on the grass with laughter.

A goblin voice broke the silence. "Guide us oh wise Coranaid. Masters of all things. Hear our call."

Nyree tore her gaze away from the painting, catching a brief glimpse of blue in the corner of her eye. The others were crowded at the edges of the arched entrance to the hall, listening intently for what followed. Finally, they might get some answers about the enemy they were chosen to defeat.

Nyree glanced quickly back to the painting and, yes, there it was. Right at the edge of the group of goblins. An imp. Peering closer, Nyree could see the superb detailing on the face. It was a perfect likeness of her brother in imp form. Stifling a gasp of surprise Nyree turned back toward the great hall. This was a puzzle she should consider later.

The great hall was packed with goblins. All of them, luckily, facing away from the entrance. Each one stared in awed silence at the dais at the far end of the room and the scene taking place upon it.

The goblin leader, in robes of blood red, was kneeling in front of an ornate stone plinth. Hovering just above this was a sphere of utter darkness. Deep within its seething mass of blackness was a spark of sickly green.

"Is your mission complete?" The green spark pulsated in time to the hissing voice from the sphere.

"Better than expected, Master Sarvar." The lead goblin grovelled as he spoke. "Not only have we captured the teacher, Malachite, but indeed the chosen ones themselves have been captured."

"We are pleased," the voice hissed. If this was its happy voice, Nyree feared to imagine its fury. "Hold them there, alive and healthy. When the time arrives, we shall come to claim them."

"I don't like the sound of this." Elias whispered in Nyree's ear. "Let's get going while we can."

"Fools," screamed the voice suddenly, "they are escaping!"

"Run!" yelled Nyree, all attempts at stealth forgotten.

"I had a silence glamour on us, I swear!" Elias grabbed Perjink and sprinted after Faltha, who was now a streak of light darting up the corridor and toward the exit.

Even the noise of Malachite's clattering footfalls didn't drown out the din of pursuing goblins as the great hall emptied itself in chase.

They hurtled through hallways, as fast as fear. Rounding a bend, Elias flung Perjink forward yelling, "Malachite!"

Malachite half-turned and caught the terrified trow, who was practically hiding inside himself. At the same moment, Elias leaped at the wall, executing a deft flip and threw a bottle back around the corner. Twisting gracefully, he righted himself, landed in the tunnel and continued to run without missing a beat.

"Glue-trap," he called to Nyree. "Should slow them down a bit. How're you doing?"

Nyree, not blessed with her brother's magical condition, just nodded and kept running.

They burst out of the passage into a huge cavern with an enormous carved gateway. The way out.

In the middle of the courtyard Malachite was crouched in a battle stance, facing off the large squad of goblin guards blocking their escape. Nyree started forward to join the battle, then stumbled as chill realisation struck her. Elias wasn't following.

She whipped around to see Elias held tightly from behind by a goblin guard. A wicked knife was pressed against her brother's throat.

"Sorry, Nyree." Although Elias held himself rigidly still, there was a tremble in his voice. "Didn't even think to check if there was one hiding by the door."

Hot fury exploded through Nyree. It drowned out everything else in the world except herself, Elias, and the goblin. The steady slap-crack and cries of pain, as Malachite smashed a way through to the exit, faded into irrelevance. In her mind's eye, Nyree saw herself tearing the goblin apart with magic. Burning it to death with terrible fire. Dragging it home to torture forever for even trying to hurt her brother.

She glanced down to see her hand lifting. A newly formed fireball flared in it, blinding with hate. Nyree steadied herself to unleash the magic, bring flaming vengeance against the goblin.

No one was going to hurt *her* brother. She wouldn't allow it. She'd burn them all alive or tear the hillside down on their heads. She'd—

Kill everyone with her fury. The goblins, Faltha, Perjink, herself, and Elias into the bargain. Maybe Malachite would survive. Maybe. That would be the end of everything. There would be no one left to stand against the enemy.

This was what the banshee warned them about. Because she loved her brother, she'd blindly destroy everything.

What then? Leave Elias to his fate? No, never that. Not even if the fate of the whole world rested on her doing that. There had to be an option three.

Her eyes narrowed coldly. The fireball was too large. It would tear through the goblin and Elias in one. Nyree focussed her magic concentrating the power into a tight beam of destruction. If Malachite had taught her anything it was the value of precision.

Then a moment of clarity. Like a movie in her mind, she could see this playing out. The needle point of energy flying to its target. The goblin flinching, twisting away. A slice and a pull. Elias, bleeding from the neck, being dragged into the path of the flames. Screaming. Horror.

Death wasn't the answer. How could it be?

She snapped back to the present. The fire vanished like it had never been, but her fury didn't dissipate with the flames. Comprehension burst from the image in Nyree's mind and the goblin's knife dissolved into dust. But Nyree's anger still had to go somewhere. She slammed her hand to the ground and with it all her will and wrath. An earthquake blast rippled through the ground.

The goblin guard holding Elias stumbled and lost his grip. Nyree could hear the other goblins thrown to the ground. The rock-fall crash of Malachite losing his footing. Elias, steady on his feet, threw the guard over his shoulder with a dimly remembered judo move then tossed him behind, into the goblins from the great hall who were now arriving.

"Go!" yelled Elias. He leaped forward and grabbed Nyree by the hand as they both fled for the exit.

They crossed the threshold at a sprint, Nyree and Elias in the lead followed closely by Perjink and Faltha. Malachite, acting as a rear guard, threw back the first few goblins to recover from Nyree's earthquake, then he too stepped out to freedom. With a burst of desperate magic Nyree slammed the massive gates closed.

"Malachite! Block the doors!" she yelled.

Malachite threw his weight against the doors. As the first wave of goblins struck, the gates strained dangerously outward. Elias bounded back to help Malachite keep them closed. The goblins crashed once more against the doors, which moved again, though not as much this time.

"Nyree." Elias grunted under the strain. "I think we're going to need something more permanent than this."

"Just a moment." Nyree stood, a single point of calm amid the chaos. "I need to think this through."

"Are you kidding?" Elias spun to put his back against the door to scowl at his sister. Another enormous crash shifted the gates again. "Feels like they've got a battering ram now. Hurry up!"

"Just drop the mountain on the faithless renegades." Perjink muttered, a few steps behind Nyree.

"I won't harm them if I don't have to." Nyree had had enough of killing. Enough violence and fury. "Trapping them in would be a death sentence. We need a better way."

The thudding of the battering ram continued relentlessly making the gates rattle on their hinges as Nyree cast around for inspiration.

"Quickly, Nyree!" Elias sounded distinctly worried now.

"Perhaps we should leave now." Malachite grunted as the door slammed against him again. "We can fight them back another day. Find a permanent solution then."

"No." Nyree allowed no argument. She was done with death. Done with chaos. "We're ending this now."

Across the quarry, Nyree found the inspiration she was after. She yelled in triumph, called up her magic to drag over a massive boulder, and planted it in front of the gates like a sentry.

"Perjink," she said softly, not taking her eyes off the stone, "could you go fetch our stuff, please? If this doesn't work, we'll need to leave in a hurry."

"Or if you take much longer," added Elias through gritted teeth.

As Perjink scurried off, Nyree started scratching a line

213

in the soil from the stone to the cliff wall near the doors. Faltha watched her for a moment, then made a similar mark from the other side of the stone, completely enclosing the gateway.

Nyree stepped carefully over and placed a hand on the boulder. She closed her eyes. Make or break time. Consciously, deliberately, she closed out distractions. The hum of Faltha's wings. The slamming on the great doors. Perjink's panicked panting. All of it dissolved into the background. There was just her and the sentry-stone. She summoned her magic.

First, a magical barrier running from the sentry stone along the lines that she and Faltha had drawn. A second layer let the sentry judge the intentions of anyone within the barrier area. The final part unified the spell, making the barrier closed to anyone with malice in mind.

Malachite, sensing the nature of the magic, looked concerned. "An interesting idea Nyree, but how will the spell be maintained once you leave here?"

"I was planning to lock the magic in place," Nyree said softly, still concentrating on holding the spell in place, "like the spells in my staff."

"I was afraid of that." Despite the constant battering, somehow Malachite still sounded like he was giving a lecture. "The trouble with that is that it still needs you to provide the magical power. In principle, it works, but your sentry will need a sorcerer to stay here to keep it working."

"But what about the cloak on the tower?"

"The brownies, Cauldron and I have been feeding it power," said Malachite. "Were we all to leave, the tower would become visible once more."

"Oh! Hang on. I know!" Elias leaped up in excitement. The next crash of the battering ram opened the gates by several centimetres before Malachite slammed them shut again.

"Sorry Mal." Elias turned back to help again.

"No," grunted Malachite, digging his feet in more firmly. "Do what you must. I can hold it."

"Nyree." Elias bounded over to his sister and the sentry rock. "You remember how imp blood can power a potion?"

"Brilliant." Nyree gritted her teeth. In her excitement, she had nearly lost concentration and let the spell crumble.

Elias fumbled in his mouth for a moment, then pulled out a tooth. "Rat-bags knocked this lose when they flung us in the cell."

He slammed his hand against the sentry rock, cracking off a chunk. He placed his tooth deep inside the fissure then stuffed the broken fragments in on top of it. Nyree's relieved smile told him that it had worked.

"Hang on. Don't seal the spell yet." Faltha flittered over to touch the sentry stone.

Nyree felt the magic shift slightly, but the spell itself was undamaged. She grinned at the faery. The sentry stone had taken on the shape of a gigantic black dog, its ferocious expression daring any to approach.

"Okay Malachite, we're ready." Nyree dropped her own magic. She felt the spell hold, powered by Elias's tooth.

"You two will need to explain this to me," said Malachite as he ran over to them. "Later," he added as the gates crashed open.

Goblins flooded out screaming battle cries.

Nyree retrieved her staff from Perjink. Despite now cowering behind her, he had managed to collect Nyree's staff, Elias's cauldron, and their other belongings.

The horde charged out from the cliff-face. Nyree held her breath, hoping that the spell would work. The goblins slammed into the invisible barrier, bouncing off and collapsing to the ground.

Nyree stepped up to the barrier, "I have enchanted this sentry to watch over Faerykirk. None may pass this barrier if they want to harm someone. You are free to leave if you want to hunt or do other peaceful things. This barrier works in both directions. From now, on nobody can visit the Faerykirk stronghold with ill-will in their hearts. You are safe from the Coranaid. You don't need to do what they say anymore."

Nyree turned to her friends. She offered Malachite a grip of her staff, then took to the air. Elias grabbed Perjink and leaped up, catching the staff then riding it like a surfboard. Faltha took her place between Nyree and Malachite, just in front of Elias.

Chapter 21

Home

The brownies had cleared away all evidence of the battle. Where the lawns were most damaged, they had added new flower beds, artfully arranged as if they had been planned all along.

Unfortunately, the welcoming and tranquil scene was disrupted by two large groups of people arguing heatedly. Something approaching battle lines were starting to form as the angry voices reached new heights.

"Oh. Not good," murmured Faltha. "They're from the Seelie Court, and I'm betting the others are Unseelies. This could get messy."

Nyree landed between the two groups on the front steps of the tower. She sagged for a moment, leaning on her staff. Malachite offered her an arm for support, which Nyree gently pushed away. She smiled wearily at him. She was grateful for his help, but she had to face these faeries herself.

Nyree swayed on her feet as she regarded the angry horde. As she drew breath to speak when Elias slipped under Malachite's arm and stood protectively between his sister and the assembled faeries.

"Enough!" His voice, amplified by glamour, echoed off the outer walls. "It's been a tough day. I'm sure you know why. Thank you all for coming, now please, go away."

"Young master," the leader of the Seelie group turned to Elias and bent to one knee. "I am Mathan, knight of the Great Seelie Court of Fae. We were sent to greet you on your return to the tower, and then thereafter to meet with you at some greater length to discuss a formal alliance between the tower and the Court. Upon our arrival, we discovered these loathsome creatures lurking. Please allow us the honour of evicting them from your home."

"Loathsome creatures?" Mathan's counterpart stood tall and proud, her velvet voice edged with steel and death, "How dare you speak of me so?" She turned to address Elias. "I am Eolande, knight of the Unseelie Court, as well he knows. This foul disrespect for free-thinking faeries is typical of the Seelie Court, although I would have hoped that their emissary could muster at least some courtesy. I, and my companions are here to welcome you back from your rescue mission. With your permission, I would like to debrief our agent Perjink, who we hope has been of some help. We are also here to offer you any further assistance that might be required, although I see that you have matters well in hand. Finally, we come to extend a hand of friendship from the Great Unseelie Court of Fae to you, the master and mistress of the Tower."

As she finished speaking, Eolande made a low bow. A flourish of her hands sent her long purple cloak billowing behind her in a most dramatic fashion. The movement was so natural that it seemed accidental when the hem landed on Mathan's face.

"Did you not hear me?" Elias's furious eyes backed up his icy tone. "I said, we're tired. Please, leave. I won't ask again."

Mathan furiously tugged the cloak from his face. "Young master, if I may—"

"My apologies for the intrusion," interrupted Eolande. "Please, be at rest. Perjink can summon us when you are rested and ready for guests." Eolande straightened up and turned with another elegant flip of her cloak, which once again caught Mathan's face. Gesturing to her retinue, she strode smoothly from the courtyard.

Mathan looked as though he was about to speak again but Malachite's menacing rumble dissuaded him. Bowing to Nyree and Malachite he too turned and left.

"Sorry about him." Faltha landed on Nyree's shoulder. "He's not exactly a people person. Tends to stay rigidly on mission, regardless of what's going on. He's really not a bad guy, though."

"Stuck up like the rest of you." Perjink scurried from behind Nyree, looking up at Faltha. "Although, in fairness, he's probably the worst."

"Please, stop." Nyree couldn't take much more of this. "I just want to go home."

"We are home." Malachite's warm rumble was filled

with relief.

"No," said Elias. He held Nyree's free hand. "Not yet. We're not home yet."

Nyree let her hand slip from her staff, leaving it standing in place on the steps of the tower. Slowly, she and Elias walked across the courtyard, through the outer gate, and into the forest.

∞⊰⊱∞

"You alright?" Elias asked quietly.

They had just left the forest trails, stepping out into the maintained order of Duloch Park. Elias was struck by the wild normality. The paved pathways and cut grass. Its painted fences and well-kept climbing-frames. They seemed at once soul-crushingly dull and yet comforting, safe, and homely.

"Yeah," Nyree mumbled in reply, then after a moment: "No. I don't know."

Nyree said nothing else for a while. As the silence dragged on, Elias opened his mouth to speak. He shut it again, cocking his head slightly to the side. He looked at his sister for a moment, who was trudging wearily onward, gaze fixed firmly on the ground. He nodded once to himself and carried on walking in silence.

Their feet turned unbidden toward the play-area at the edge of the park nearest home. As they sat on the swings, Nyree finally spoke.

"I thought I was going to lose you there, you know."

"Yeah, it got pretty tense." Elias pretended a

220

nonchalance that neither of them believed.

"I almost threw that fireball…"

"Spotted that." Elias nodded slightly. "I think the goblin did too. I felt his grip shifting. Figured the wee toe-rag wanted me as a shield."

"Huh, that was exactly what I imagined would happen. It was terrible. I saw myself burning you to ash with my magic. I couldn't stop it. I just couldn't…" Nyree's voice cracked, ended in a squeak.

"But you did stop it," Elias interrupted, trying to break her out of the panicked memories. "That earthquake was genius. Saved us all with that one. See? This was what the banshee was on about. It could have gone a million different ways. You might have just saved me from one goblin but left us trapped by the whole horde. Obviously, you could have, you know, not helped me. Instead, you came up with something awesome that saved us all. You got us all out and as far as I could see, didn't even kill a single goblin into the bargain."

"But it could have gone so horribly wrong." Hysteria rose in Nyree's voice again. "I almost…"

"But you didn't."

"But I could have…"

"But you didn't." Elias was so firm that after a moment Nyree nodded once and said no more.

A few minutes passed silently. They swung with no enthusiasm, just meditative monotony.

Elias sighed. For some reason, he wasn't really troubled by what had happened. Sure, it had been a close thing. Not actually that close, though. It could have gone badly, but then so could all those falls out of trees or bad dives at the pool. That time he'd smacked a moving car with his bike was definitely closer. Overlooking the whole goblins and magic theme, the danger itself was barely unusual. Nyree seemed way more upset than he was. Did she think she was a bad person, just because she could have made a mistake?

"Dad would know what to say." He said at last.

"Yeah, like we could tell him!" Nyree laughed joylessly. "What would we say? 'Hi Dad, you know that whole sleepover thing? Well, that was a lie. We really went to rescue our alive-statue friend from some goblins. Don't worry though, it all worked out fine. Although I did nearly kill Elias.' That'll be fun."

"Well, yeah. I mean, I know we can't tell him." Elias rolled his eyes. How Nyree could be so smart and so completely dopey at the same time was a mystery to him. "But if he *was* in on the whole thing, he'd know what to say."

"If only he was in on it." Nyree slipped off the swing. "Come on, let's go home."

⋙✦⋘

As the front door slammed, Elias yelled, "Dad! We're home."

"Oh, hi kids." Their Dad's head appeared around the kitchen door. "Have fun?"

"Yeah, it was fine," answered Nyree. She walked heavily up the stairs to her room and closed the door softly behind her. Sanctuary. Home at last. She sank onto her cabin bed's sofa. There was a gentle knock on the door.

"You alright, my girl?" her Dad sounded a little worried, but then, he always did.

"I'm fine Dad, really."

He slipped into the room, only opening the door the bare minimum, and squatted down next to Nyree. It seemed he didn't believe her.

"Did something happen?"

"No, not really." Nyree smiled weakly. "Well, I mean, stuff happened, obviously. But nothing bad happened. Nothing you need to know about, anyway."

"Okay, cool. So, some unimportant, not really stuff, stuff happened. Glad we got that sorted." Her Dad stood up, half turning to leave. "You know you can tell me anything, right? If you want to talk about it."

"I know Dad." Nyree attempted another smile, then after a moment leaped up and hugged him fiercely.

"Okay, my girl," he said gently. He lowered himself onto Nyree's sofa, carefully maintaining the hug all the way. "Okay. You know you can tell me *anything*."

Tears filled Nyree's eyes. Not *anything*. No. She couldn't tell him this. It wasn't the goblins and magic and stuff. That was just unbelievable. That she could handle. What she couldn't manage was telling him that she'd lied.

Her dad twisted until he was looking at her. The tiny muscles around his eyes twitched and danced. Like he was trying to look straight through her eyes and directly read her brain.

"I think something unusual happened. I think it

scared you, and however you handled it, you're worried that you didn't get it right, and that has you all twisted up inside."

Tears were running freely down Nyree's face now, but her dad wasn't finished yet.

"Thing is, though," he continued, "that's where you've gone wrong. I don't know exactly what all this is about, but I *know* that you did the right thing." He held up a hand to forestall any argument. "I know you did the right thing because I know *you*. I know you and I trust you. You have a good head, and a good heart. You did the right thing and I'm proud of you."

Nyree smiled through her tears. She felt a lightness inside, like a tiny black hole that she hadn't even noticed before had suddenly evaporated.

Then her dad chuckled to himself. "Which makes me kind of proud of me too. After all you weren't born this awesome!"

Nyree snorted a laugh, which turned into a grimace as a snot-bubble ruined the whole moment. A tissue appeared, almost magically, in her dad's hand and she cleaned herself up.

He slipped out of her arms and stood to go. At the door he paused then added, "Of course, if it was drugs or smoking, you're basically grounded for life…" He grinned, and Nyree figured that he knew it wasn't either of those.

The smoke alarm outside Nyree's bedroom shrieked into life, warning of a raging inferno, or possibly just burned toast.

Her dad's eyes widened in shock. "Damn it, I left the

224

dinner on the hob!"

He leaped out of the room as if he could move quickly enough to un-burn the food. Nyree lay back on her cushions smiling to herself.

Chapter 22

Foreboding

All was stillness at the top of the tower of sorcery. Malachite looked out over the tower's grounds and the forest beyond. A heavy frown creased his craggy brow, but no movement suggested any signs of life. When alone, Malachite didn't bother with breathing. Being a creature of stone and sorcery, he had no use for breath. Other people seemed to find this disturbing so, when in company, he pretended. But on nights like this, when the moon was full and the battlements empty, he was free to be just himself. Almost.

"Good evening, Cauldron." Malachite spoke without turning around.

Cauldron clambered on silent feet over the parapet. "How do you hear me coming?" he grumped. "I've managed to sneak up on bats in the jungle canopy. I swear I'm even quieter on stone. How do you know?"

"We are carved of the same rock, the tower and I. It

tells me everything."

"Tells you everything? It's a tower for goodness' sake." Cauldron scoffed.

"And yet you consider me alive." Malachite looked thoughtfully at Cauldron.

"Aren't you?"

"No more than the tower. No more than a mountain." Malachite gazed into the distance again. "No less than the world."

"So, what does the tower tell you, then?"

"That all is not well." Malachite sighed, an affectation which he rather enjoyed. "There is a storm building, and I fear it will break before we are ready. The goblins were sent by the Coranaid. That is now clear. Already they strike at us, and yet all we know is rumour and the barest hint of legend. Already they are strong. I know that much. They terrified the goblins into obedience."

"Terrified the goblins? That's not a good sign." Cauldron made a thoughtful clicking with his mouth. "Do you think we should move up the schedule?"

"I think we need to completely change our plans." Malachite stared at Cauldron, awaiting an argument.

"Oh?" Cauldron knew better.

"I want to turn this place into a fortress. We are wide open here. I cannot defend Nyree and Elias in this place as it is, and that is paramount. They are the future of us all."

"I have never once doubted it, my friend." Cauldron shifted, looking down the tower. "Perhaps might and weaponry are not the answer. Could it be that knowledge

228

and wisdom are the stronger path?"

"They are already working as hard as they can." A warm pride spread through Malachite's voice. "Nyree has learned sorcery and spell craft far faster than I had dreamed possible and Elias rarely fails to astonish me. But they are still young. Wisdom takes time and that appears to be in shorter supply than we had hoped."

"I did not mean just the children." Cauldron shuffled his feet uncomfortably. "Throw open the gates to all who wish to learn magic. Build of this place a centre of learning, a blazing beacon against the night that is to come."

"And yet, that night is drawing in upon us." Malachite studied his fists. "The prophecy was never clear. Not on the danger. Not on how to counter it. Indeed, until it had happened, I did not know that the prophecy had intended for two to be chosen. Events are moving too fast, and I cannot see to what end."

"Then we must forge that end. You and I." Cauldron turned to look straight at Malachite. "If we cannot see the way we must go, then we must use what prophecy and chance have given us and create the future ourselves."

"I don't know that that is for us to do." Malachite's head bowed, not meeting Cauldron's eyes. "I fear that burden is for the children to bear. That it must be their choices which create the future for us all."

"How can we put that on them?" There was a tremble in Cauldron's voice, "It's too much. Too much for anyone. How can we dare place that burden on children?"

"I think fate has placed it on them, whether we like it

or not." Malachite stared out at the forest, "All that there is, is to help them as we may."

"That is all there is." He added in a whisper which was carried off by the breeze.

The End.

Read on for a sneak preview of

THE FALL OF
WITCHES

The Wizard and the Imp Book 2

Chapter 1

School's out

Elias slipped through the press of bodies like a leaf on the breeze. It was so easy to go unnoticed that he didn't even bother with a glamour. The focus of the crowd's primal attention wasn't on him anyway. He reached the clearing in the middle just in time to see an arm raised, a fist clenched and ready to strike. With a deftly timed tap on the elbow, Elias made the punch swing wide. The bully, a hulking lump of boy, twisted slightly and took half a step forward when his knuckles failed to connect with his would -be victim. Elias gently nudged the ankle of the boy's rising foot. Tangled on his own feet, the bully fell to the ground. Elias helped him down, making sure that he landed hard, but not too hard.

Twenty boys held their breath, stilling the ritual chant of: "Fight! Fight! Fight!"

Stuart Wylie, the notorious bully from primary 7, climbed to his feet. His outraged face was flushed red with fury. His right fist, knuckles skinned and bleeding from the fall, shook with the urgent need to smash someone's teeth.

"What's your problem wee man?" yelled Stuart as he turned to loom threateningly over Elias.

"I guess that I'm just too awesome." Elias grinned as irritatingly as he could manage. "Oh, sorry, you meant, like, specifically."

Stuart swung a heavy right-hook, which Elias avoided with a slight tilt of his head. Almost as if he was exaggeratedly thinking about the question.

"Well," Elias let his schoolbag slip from his shoulder and stepped to the left, "I don't like bullies."

Stuart unleashed a vicious upper-cut. Elias leaned back slightly and the blow whispered past. With a twinkle in his eye, he licked Stuart's wrist as it went by.

"Ugh," Stuart snatched his hand back as if it had been stung. He wiped it on his other sleeve and glared at Elias, "What's wrong with you?"

Elias took another step, forcing Stuart to turn.

"What were you wanting from him anyway?" Elias nodded at the primary 4 boy who Stuart had been about to clobber.

"He had a bag of sweets." Stuart launched a volley of quick punches, though somehow none landed. "He didn't give me them when I asked."

"He..." in his surprise, Elias stopped moving. Taking advantage of this Stuart stepped in, grabbed Elias's shoulder and thumped him in the gut as hard as he could. Under Elias's shirt, thankfully out of everyone's sight, his skin flashed a deep blue as his magical imp strength absorbed the blow.

"When I ask for things," Stuart didn't seem to notice that his punch hadn't had the expected effect, "you give them to me. Or you get hit." He struck again.

"Hey," said Elias breezily, "those were not bad. With a bit of work, I might feel them next time."

There was a nervous chuckle at that from the group of boys still surrounding them. Stuart straightened up and took a step back. The red on his face this time had an embarrassed tint.

"I'm gonna kill you," growled Stuart through gritted teeth.

"Really?" Elias feigned shock, "Over a bag of sweets? If you want them that much - take them."

Elias produced a tube of mints from his pocket and flicked them at Stuart's chest. He hoped that nobody would notice his fingers flickering to blue and back as he let go. The mints slammed into Stuart with a surprisingly loud thud, knocking him backward. The bag that Elias had dropped at the start of the fight was perfectly placed to trip Stuart and for the second time in five minutes the bully crashed to the ground.

"Forester!" The headmaster, his face a mask of rage, was storming down the path toward Elias. As he approached, the crowd of boys evaporated like a morning mist.

Elias rolled his eyes and sighed, then turned to the headmaster. "Yes, mister Glaspy?"

"Don't you 'yes, mister Glaspy' me, boy," roared Mr Glaspy. "Fighting again, Forester? And who have we picked on this time?" Mr Glaspy glanced down to see Stuart struggling to disentangle his feet from the straps of Elias's bag. "Oh, it's you."

"Sorry, sir," Elias mumbled, trying to look and sound contrite.

"Why is it, Elias," Mr Glaspy seemed to deflate as he asked, "that you insist on picking fights with the biggest bullies in the playground?"

"Well, sir, it's like this: we had a bit of a misunderstanding about..."

"Never mind, Elias," Mr Glaspy interrupted, "I don't really want to hear it. Go to my office now, both of you. I'll be along shortly."

∽∾⊰⊱∽∾

Nyree sat with her chin resting on her left hand. The pencil in her right hand was vaguely wandering across the paper - doodling as if on its own. She was idly musing about what she was going to work on with Malachite. This was the last day of school before the October break. Two weeks off to spend at the Tower. Nyree was looking forward to having the time to study some more advanced magic. Since the start of term, her magical studies had been restricted to short exercises. Malachite insisted that having a well-rounded education was essential to a wizard. So, the term had crawled by glacially, with school-work dragging into homework. Even her greedily snatched visits to the Tower, when she could squeeze one in between homework and dinner-time, provided little relief. More often than not,

Malachite insisted that she spend her little time working on focus and mindfulness exercises. Despite her begging to learn new skills, he was mountainously unmovable on the issue.

Never mind that the Enemy, predicted in prophecy, was apparently moving against them far sooner than Malachite had expected. They had discovered over the summer that the enemy was the Coranaid, a group of evil sorcerers who had the power to hear any words spoken, no matter how quietly and no matter where in the world they were said.

Malachite had at least allowed her to borrow some books for some bed-time reading — only once he'd been satisfied that she wouldn't break the spines. It wasn't much, but it was something at least. Something to help get her ready.

The Coranaid terrified Nyree. Their power made them practically invincible — how could you plan and execute an attack against creatures who could hear everything you say? There would be no element of surprise where the Coranaid were concerned. They were beaten before by the invention of writing. It was only then that the ancients had the tools to move against the Coranaid. Even then, they weren't destroyed — only banished to some darksome trap. Well, they were out now and Nyree had a feeling that they would have learned some new tricks in the thousands of years since. To beat them again would need something new, something special, something...

"Miss Forester, we are waiting," Nyree's teacher, Ms Lockart, was wearing her 'look how even-tempered I'm being' face.

"For what, Ms Lockart?" Nyree came to her senses as the words left her mouth. A desperate flush of embarrassment coloured her cheeks as a titter of laughter ran around the classroom.

"Your answer, Nyree." Reasonably enough, Ms Lockart didn't look impressed, "We are waiting for your answer."

"X equals thirty-seven," whispered Crissa Storer from the row behind Nyree.

"Um, X equals thirty-seven?" answered Nyree hopefully.

She didn't need the giggles of her classmates to work out that this was not the right answer. The look on Ms Lockart's face was quite enough confirmation.

"And that's all you've managed to find out about Peru, is it Nyree?" Ms Lockart looked like she'd reached the crumbling edge of her patience.

The mortified glow on Nyree's cheeks spread to her neck and forehead. She looked down at her desk as if salvation, or at least a hiding place, might be found there. Her textbook was opened to a page with a picture of a towering plant. That had led her mind to wander to the Tower, which had brought her into musing about the Coranaid, which had... Nyree dragged her attention back to the page, and quickly scanned it for information.

"The Puya Raimondii or Queen of the Andes grows there. It's the largest species of bromeliad in the world."

"That's better," Ms Lockart took a breath and forced

a tired smile. "Now, I think we should move on while we're ahead."

"That wee… urgh!" shrieked Amy as she and Nyree stepped out of the classroom. "What on earth did you listen to her for anyway?"

"Wasn't thinking." Nyree had a faraway look as she grabbed her bag and coat.

"I'm not sure that's the problem," mused Amy as they walked out together. "I think you think too much, just, about the wrong things."

Nyree found it amazing to think that she'd only known Amy for eight weeks. The two girls had hit it off almost immediately, when they met before the summer holiday. Despite not seeing each other for the entire break they had picked up their friendship without missing a beat this term. Since the end of week one, Amy and Nyree had been almost inseparable. The next two weeks would be hard. The prospect of not seeing Amy every day left Nyree feeling a little bit small, and quite a bit lost. However, the magic called to her, and she couldn't miss the chance to learn more.

"Hmm? Yeah, I guess so,"

"You see, there you go again. You're away with the faeries."

"If only," sighed Nyree. Her eyes widened as she realised what she had just said. She shot a quick glance at

Amy, who was looking at her thoughtfully.

"What on earth do you mean by that?"

"Nothing," said Nyree hastily, "nothing at all."

"If you say so," said Amy, "but, just so you know, I'm not convinced."

"Oh look: it's the weirdos!" Apparently not content with humiliating Nyree in class, Crissa Storer was back for more.

Crissa Storer was like the anti-Amy. Within about fifty milliseconds of meeting, she and Nyree knew they would loathe each other forever. Somehow, every single thing that Nyree did was cause for Crissa to bully, belittle or harass her. For Nyree's part Crissa's every act was as irritant as an onion contact-lens. It seemed more than a little unfair to Nyree that she would already have two mortal enemies in the world: one who she barely knew, intent on socially murdering her at school; the other who she did not know at all, and who probably planned to actually kill her.

"Oh no. It's her again." Amy seemed to shrink into herself.

"Just keep walking." Nyree held herself unnaturally straight and quickened her pace. "Don't even look at her."

"Lucky for you two Halloween is coming up," Crissa went on with a sneer, "the one night a year when you don't need to wear costumes."

Nyree swallowed hard and drew a trembling breath. She looked down at her twitching fingers. Tiny sparks of lightning had begun to dance between their tips, begging to be unleashed. She let the breath out slowly and held the magic in. Nyree glanced at her friend to see how she was doing.

Amy had ducked her head even further, her mousey brown hair fell over her face, almost, but not quite, hiding the glow of a blush that was highlighting her dusting of freckles. Amy's eyes shone bright with a muster of tears that were threatening to fall at any moment.

Magic boiled in a cauldron of hate inside Nyree. She fought to hold it down. Giving Nyree a hard time was one thing, but she couldn't stand to see her friends hurt. She turned to Amy and, voice tight with restraint, asked, "Do you hear that chittering, Aimes? What kind of insect do you think it is?"

Amy's head snapped round toward Nyree. Surprise battled with the hurt on her face, won control of her forehead and lifted her eyebrows.

A little more control edged into Nyree's voice as she continued. "I was thinking it could be a northern dung beetle. It would explain the smell, at least." Nyree wrinkled her nose as she looked at Crissa.

Amy choked out a strained laugh and tension leaked from her shoulders. Nyree offered Amy her hand and the two girls walked off without another glance at Crissa.

They stopped to look back when they heard a shriek followed closely by a splash and another shriek. Elias was running toward them wearing a cheerful grin and leaving chaos in his wake. Behind him Crissa was standing ankle deep in a puddle and liberally sprayed with muddy water. Next to her Stuart Wylie was picking himself and his scooter up from the grass. They were both yelling angrily at each other.

"What on earth happened back there?" asked Amy as Elias reached them.

"Had a clumsy moment." Elias's grin was almost unnaturally wide. "I was running to catch up and accidentally bumped that girl into a puddle. Stuart was going through it at the time and she got a bit splashed. I think she knocked him off his scooter."

"Oh, how unfortunate," Nyree grinned back at him.

"You know," Amy looked thoughtful again, "your clumsy moments seem remarkably well timed."

"Yeah, maybe that's my super-power." Elias chuckled. "Just call me 'Accident Man'. Here to save the day by crashing into stuff."

They wandered through the school gates, which in Nyree's mind officially started the holiday. Elias and Amy were busily wittering to each other. It seemed that Elias's 'Accident Man' idea had sparked their imaginations and they were engrossed in cooking up a wild tale of his adventures. Nyree allowed her attention to drift to the magic she might get to learn over the next two weeks. Her encounter with Crissa Storer had left her with an urge to learn something about transfiguration. Aside from exacting a poetic revenge on the school hate-mongers, Nyree was sure that being able to transform things into something more immediately useful would be a helpful skill to have. On the other hand, some means of silent, instant communication should maybe be the top priority. Combating the Coranaid ought to top any to-do list they might make.

Of course, Malachite had other ideas. His were more along the lines of magical fortifications to the tower and other boring things like that. Nyree chuckled to herself at that, amazed at the notion that doing magic of any kind could seem boring.

"Hello? Earth to Nyree." Amy's voice snapped Nyree's attention back to the present just before Elias's gentle punch to the shoulder would have.

"Oh. Sorry, Amy." Nyree smiled at her friend. "daydreaming again."

"Is Fairyland nice this time of year?"

"It's pretty much like here. Hang on. What?"

"Never mind, Nyree." Amy chuckled, shaking her head slightly. "Anyway, can you come round to mine this afternoon, or do you have other stuff on?"

"We, ah. We kind of..." Nyree suddenly found her shoes surprisingly interesting.

"It's all right, Nyree." Amy smiled at her. "You're allowed to have other things to do. Tomorrow then?"

"Actually, Mum and Dad have us pretty busy for the whole holiday." Elias interrupted before Nyree could answer.

"Oh, okay then." Amy swallowed and bit her lip. "Well, you know where I am if you get a spare moment." She turned to go.

"Amy, wait."

"What?" Amy whispered like she was struggling to make any sound at all.

"I'm sorry. It's just that Mum and Dad seem to have this idea that we can't occupy ourselves. We're lucky we don't have laminated timetables. I'll be round as soon as I can, okay. Promise."

Amy turned to face Nyree, a forced smile trying to play on her lips. "Try not to have too much fun without me, yeah?"

"As if!"

They hugged briefly then Amy turned and crossed the road. Nyree and Elias turned in the opposite direction and started heading for home, and the Tower of Magic beyond.

Acknowledgements

It has been a long road between the beginnings of telling this story and the book you now hold in your hands. Unsurprisingly, many people have helped make it what it is.

First, I'd like to thank the children at Carnegie Primary School in Dunfermline. Over the years they have been extremely patient test subjects who have let me try out several ideas to see what works.

A massive thank-you to Isla Fergusson, beta-reader extraordinaire and outstanding supporter of the school's resident Library Troll.

My thanks to Rebecca Wojturska, whose editorial advice whipped the manuscript into rather more usable shape.

While we're on Rebeccas, I owe a huge thank you to Becky Salter, rising star artist and the most patient of illustrators.

To Naomi Farmer, dear friend and unflinching supporter. I really can't thank you enough for not saying 'don't be stupid' all those years ago when I said I was writing a book. Going above and beyond, as usual, Naomi stuck to her guns even after I proudly showed her what turned out to be a *very* rough first draft.

Naomi is also the person who introduced me to my

wife. A debt I will never fully repay. One thing leading to another, as they do, I can say with all honesty, and some seriousness: Naomi, all this is essentially your fault!

That brings us around to my darling wife, Sarah. I'll not put down here all the ways that I'm grateful for you. I'd need another several volumes, and I don't think anyone wants to read all that. Let's just say this chapter begins with you saying in all seriousness: "Yes, of course you can stay at home and write full time with no income," and ends with everything else that I value in my life.

Speaking of whom, a huge thank you to my own Ngaire and Elias. All this started with the words "tell me a pretend story, Daddy." So I did.

The vey final thank you (I promise) is to you, dear reader. The fact that you've taken a chance on a first-time author earns you my eternal gratitude. Given that you've made it this far (I assume you're not just peeking) suggests that you enjoyed the book. I am glad because this story, and those that follow, are for you.

About the author

Brandon lives in Dunfermline, with his wife and two children. Before he wrote stuff, he was variously a software engineer, computer game developer, electronic engineer, inventor, yarn spinner (as in wool) and fencing coach.

These days, he divides his time between volunteering as Library Troll at the local primary school, roaming the hills for good locations for stories, and writing down whatever comes into his head.

Lightning Source UK Ltd.
Milton Keynes UK
UKHW041828061221
395174UK00001B/13